Mike Robbins is a journalist turned development worker. He is also the author *of Even the Dead are Coming* (2009), a memoir of Sudan; *Crops and Carbon* (2011), on agriculture and climate change; two other works of fiction, *The Lost Baggage of Silvia Guzmán* (2014) and *Three Seasons* (2014); and *The Nine Horizons* (2014), a pen-portrait of some of the countries in which he has worked and travelled since 1987. He is currently in New York.

© Mike Robbins 2015
978-0-9914374-7-4

Third Rail Books

thirdrailbooks@gmail.com

Cover picture: Amy Rene/Shutterstock
Pawprints motif: Maximus256/Shutterstock

ACKNOWLEDGEMENTS

Warm thanks to Samuel Astbury, Rupert Dreyfus, Hazel Marsh and Harry Whitewolf for their comments on the manuscript.

T he clock struck eleven.

"Have another," said the dog's man.

"I think I shall," said his guest, who was Richard from two doors down.

The dog lay where he had for most of the evening, outside the circle of sofa and armchairs, in the space between them and the hall door, below the bookshelf with its whiff of old paper. He lay on his belly and his muzzle rested on his crossed paws. Sometimes his eyes opened briefly and he looked at his master and the guest, blinked, raised his muzzle and yawned, then lowered his head. *I do wish the old sod would get rid of him, then I could go into the garden and take a shit, goodness me I need a shit, and then sleep. Maybe I should scratch at the door.*

"He looks all right, Bazza," said Richard.

"I think he is," said Bazza. He was tall and a little bulky, a powerful build going a bit to seed. His silver hair, a little thin on top, was tied back in a ponytail and he wore a jacket of faded blue denim.

He flipped the top off a bottle of Bombardier and set it on the occasional table next to Richard, a smaller man in his thirties whose jeans and tee-shirt clashed with his steepled fingers and neatly crossed legs.

"I think he is," repeated Bazza. "He's been with me some weeks now and he seems OK. He's clearly been housetrained."

"Did the sanctuary know much about him?

"Really not much. They'd had him for a couple of months. There's not much demand for these older dogs, you know."

"Good of you to take him in then," said Richard.

Oh, don't feed my man's bloody ego, for Heaven's sake, he's already bad enough, especially since he's been shagging that red-haired postgrad with the tattoo, he thinks he's about 30 again like she is.

"Did they know why he was in the sanctuary?"

"He'd had at least two previous owners," said Bazza. "Doesn't get on with children, apparently."

Oh, well, you wouldn't have liked these kids either,

---

let me tell you. Little shits. One of them used to pull my tail and the other used to offer me biscuits and then snatch them away at the last minute. Not when their parents were around, of course. Anyway, I just gave one of the little sods a good nip on the arse, that's all. He was screaming because he didn't want to eat his greens so I snuck up and bit his arse through the gap in the wheelback chair and all hell was let loose, it was like a bomb in the street, well not quite like that, not funny that, no bombs ain't funny. Bombs. No.

The dog gave a little yelp.

"Bad dream probably," said Bazza. "They have 'em, apparently, just like us."

The dog looked up at him and licked his snout, then rested his muzzle back on his paws.

"What breed, d'ya reckon?" asked Richard.

"Dunno. Some sort of rough collie I think. You still got teaching next week? We're nearly done in Philosophy."

"One more week in our School. I'm teaching the Introduction to Politics module for year 1."

"Good lot this year?"

"Not really. Don't seem to understand the inevitability of Marxian analysis. I'm trying to demonstrate that there's no other tool."

The dog grunted.

"I expect he wants to go out," said Bazza.

"He should be lying in front of the fire really," said Richard. "That's what old dogs do as a rule."

"I haven't got a fire," said Bazza. "He could curl up in front of the fireplace though. It's Edwardian I think. Found it in a builder's yard."

"Yes, it looks quite authentic," said Richard. "Probably matches the age of the house."

Dad had a hearth, and I suppose I would have curled up in front of it just like Prince did. Can't blame him really, Dad never did dry him off after they'd been in the rain, no wonder his joints went and he was in pain, yes he really was in pain, and Sis and I were really sad but it's got to be done he said and he borrowed Mr Cooper's shotgun, the one he used to borrow in the winter for shooting crows, and he took him round the back to the vegetable garden and we heard a big crack and a yelp and then he let him have the other barrel just to make sure and Sis cried and cried, though she couldn't hear the shots of course, but I wouldn't cry because boys don't so Sis got some lemon curd and I didn't, and he wouldn't say where he'd buried him, said it was somewhere nice and peaceful and you got to get used to death 'cos it's part of life and then he said, I fancy there'll be plenty of it about inside a year or two, if last time's anything to go by. Funny, I hadn't thought on that for a while, yes there was a hearth and sometimes Dad got wood he pinched from the fox covert above Ten-Acre but Mr Cooper didn't like that, and one day Ma's brother stops by with the lorry and says, old Mrs Berry passed on and youse might as well have her weekly sack till someone comes by the yard and stops her order. So we had coal after that and Ma would get up now and then in the evening and move the glowing coals with the poker, and Sis and I got to use the toasting-fork.

"How about you?" asked Richard.

"Finished for the semester," said Bazza.

And what is a semester? Term-time was good enough for us.

"Got that monk coming though, haven't you," said Richard. "What the hell are you going to do with a monk in the house? Get up early and say Matins with him?"

"Good Lord, no," said Bazza. "He isn't that sort of monk. His name's Tshering and he lives in a monastery somewhere in the Garwhal Himalaya. He's coming over to run summer schools on the campus."

"What on?" asked Richard. "How to make yak-butter tea?"

"No, no," said Bazza. "Well, I don't think so. I think they're doing courses on Mindfulness."

"Splendid," said Richard. "It's so nice that we've moved on, so many of us, and learned to open ourselves up."

"I know," said Bazza. "I'm very proud to be a part of it all."

You pretentious nitwits. I hope this Tshering turns out to be an alcoholic with a thing for redheads. Maybe he'll enlighten her.

"So nice to be part of moving on," said Richard, "and getting rid of this stupid buttoned-up Englishness of when we were young."

You patronising little man. How the hell do you know who we were or how we thought or felt.

"The dog is looking at you," said Bazza.

"Why, so he is," said Richard. He leaned towards the dog and started clicking his tongue in encouragement. "Do you know, sometimes I think they understand everything we say?"

Bazza chuckled.

"Maybe he's an Ancient Soul," he said. "After all, we don't know who dogs really are, do we? Perhaps they're beings on the way to enlightenment."

"Ha! Maybe he is, at that."

Dog!

Actually I really, really want that shit in the garden. I should just scratch at the door and whine but that's just so servile. I know what I'll do, this never fails.

The dog stretched, yawned, and strolled over to the empty polished Edwardian grate. He lay down on his side, then curled his head around and started to lick his balls.

"I say," said Richard.

Oh, that feels good. Better wait till I go to bed to do it properly though. You don't want to waste it, like that stupid Jack Russell that Professor Courtney's wife walks by the lake. Don't know how he can possibly enjoy it. Or what he's fantasizing about. Well really, what sort of sexual fantasy do you have if you're a Jack Russell, I mean you can't exactly go round mounting Irish wolfhounds, can you. Mind you, Jack Russells, no class really.

"Are you sure he's an ancient soul?" asked Richard, a little nervously.

"No," said Bazza. Then: "Damned dog."

Bit closer to the mark there, Bazza.

"I think I'd better get my head down, anyway," said Richard. "Thanks for the drink, Bazza. Don't worry about Ellen. I'm sure you'll settle out of court in the end."

"I do hope so," said Bazza.

They stood, and went to the door. The dog heard it close, and the scrunch of Richard's feet on the gravel. Bazza came back in.

"Lot of class you got sometimes, you mangy mutt," he said.

Speak for yourself, you randy old hippie. And I'm English, so I'm a mongrel, not a mutt.

"I suppose you'd better get out there and take a dump," said Bazza. "I'd take you for a walk, but I'm knackered. Come on."

He led the dog through to the kitchen and opened the door into the back garden.

"OK, go shit," he said mildly.

Go and *shit. Get it right.*

He watched the dog trot out into the garden, tail swaying gently this way and that. The dog turned round a few times in the pool of light from the kitchen window, then slid into the shadows. Bazza shrugged. It was not a cold night. *As long as I remember to let him in later. But OK, he'll bark at the door. Funny he doesn't whine to be let in, like most dogs do. Always the one bark.* He poured a drink, climbed the stairs, washed and put on his dressing-down, then sat on his bed. As he did so he noticed a long red

14

hair on the pillow on the other side of the bed. He smiled, picked it up with thumb and forefinger and dropped it on the floor. Then he picked up the tablet on his bedside table and opened his email. There was one from his sister. He frowned as he read it. "We are coming on the third," she had written. "Clarissa has an appointment with the speech therapist at County General. She's doing quite well really but we wish things would go better. Anyway, shall we call by? We can have tea. How are things with Ellen?"

He pressed reply.

"3rd OK. Things with Ellen aren't."

He lay back on his pillow and tapped an address into the browser with his first and second fingers. The page loaded. He thought for a minute, then clicked on the link *Hairy Desi teen*. She was a bit pudgy though, so he pressed the Back button and typed: *hairy milf*. This brought up a better selection. He reached across for the glass of amaro he had poured himself in the kitchen.

Outside, the dog slunk to the end of the garden; then, standing in the shadow of Bazza's prized rhododendron bush, he turned to see if the kitchen light had been switched off. It had, so he lifted his leg on the root of the bush. *My goodness, that feels good*, he thought. Satisfied for the moment, he lowered his leg. Time for a shit. He stretched luxuriously and then made his way to the back of the bush, where it butted onto the wall that divided the garden from the neighbours behind. Here, the wooden panel fence to the right had been damaged in the equinoctial gales of the autumn before, and replaced with a length of planking that was an inch or two above the ground. The dog pawed at the ground below the planking until he found the site of his previous excavations, then laid his head close to the ground and wriggled slowly through, his rear legs stretched out behind him. Easy does it, he told himself. Don't get a splinter in your back. He came out into the neighbour's garden, which he liked; it was unkempt and full of bushes and the grass was long, and full of small furry animals that sometimes passed in front of him, causing him to dart in pursuit before he remembered that he had nothing against them. The lights on the ground floor were off, but there was a dim light behind the curtains on the first floor. The dog was not concerned, but moved slowly through the long grass.

That scent.

The dog's ears pricked up and he dropped on his belly. A few yards away the long grass wavered in the breeze. A shadow came clear from the dark area around the bins at the back of the house and trotted across the mown area immediately behind the back door. Then it sensed the dog, and stopped, one front paw raised, its own ears pricked up, and sniffed the air. The dog growled quietly and the vixen turned its head toward him; then turned and slunk out through the side-passage, unconcerned.

The bedroom window opened and a slice of light lanced across the garden. The dog lowered himself further into the grass.

"Fox I think... What? No, gone. Yes, Katie's chickens, I remember; fearful mess."

The window closed and the path of light fell back, leaving the grass in darkness.

Yes, they got ours too. I was away by then. Wanted to work on the farm but Cooper wouldn't have me, I'm not having that lad, his dad's bad enough, whole family's a bad lot if you ask me. Then he gave Dad his cards. Well at least we got eggs, Ma says, then a fucking fox gets the chickens. I'm fresh in uniform and square-bashing all day long and that bastard Sergeant Fitch is picking on me and I gets a letter, Dad lost his job and then they lost the chickens. I'm an old dog but I've got my claws and a bit of weight, I won't go for a vixen in case she got cubs, but if I catch a dog fox in the garden I'll tear the little sod limb from limb.

The dog moved on slowly through the long grass. At the far side of the garden was a chest-high paling fence; this time it stretched all the way to the back wall, but the long grass had hidden the effects of neglect, and there was a small hole at the bottom of the fence, easy for a fox and just large enough for an enterprising dog. He closed his eyes and wriggled through, putting one front paw ahead of him and pulling the other through the hole by pressing his paw hard up against his belly. The two rear legs and the tail followed after. He looked right, towards the back of Richard's house. He had to be careful here as the garden had little natural growth; there was a wooden deck immediately behind the house, then a patio of crazy paving that stretched most of the way down the garden. *God, I hate his garden as much as I do him. Jeans with creases ironed in, garden with no grass, just nice crazy paving.* The kitchen light was on; the dog could see Richard filling a water-bottle to take upstairs. Then the light went off. *He'll go to the bathroom before he goes to bed.* He did. The light came on behind the frosted window through which Richard would see nothing. *Now.* The dog slid onto the centre of the crazy paving, looking left and right to make sure he was right in the middle; then crouched and shat. *Goodness me that feels good. Oooh, a big one. Nice big steaming dog turd right in the middle of prissy little Richard's "garden". Apply Marxian analysis to* that, *dickhead.* He waited until he was sure the last of the turd had been evacuated, then lowered his tail and ran for the hole in the fence at the back. Once through into the overgrown garden next door, he sat down and panted for a while, his tongue hanging out.

He became aware of another scent, different from the fox's; also that he was being watched. A shape detached itself from the top of the wall at the back of the garden and fell on its feet two or three yards away, then came towards him. He stood up and faced the creature and emitted a low warning growl. *I don't like these things. They claw at you. They can* hurt *you. The* creature looked straight back. It was big muscular old grey-and-white cat and looked set to give a good account of itself.

Two doors down someone opened a bedroom window and the light lanced across the garden, not for long – just a second or two – but it was enough to catch the dog's eyes. The cat looked into them. It arched its back; its tail stood up and its fur too and it hissed, and then it looked at the dog's eyes again and then it backed slowly away and it yowled. It yowled so loud that it split the night. It was a sound so full of fear and horror and loathing that people in the houses around must have stiffened and sprung up in bed, their bowels turned to water. *Oh God he knows*, thought the dog, *he knows what I am, that is the terror of a creature that has set eyes on the very face of hell*. He sank down on his belly, his muzzle on the ground, his body shielded by the long grass so that he could not be seen as the windows round about started to open one by one. As for the cat, as soon as it could gather its wits it fled, scrambling across the wall into the garden behind. The dog remained; it had to for a while, until the alarm was forgotten and the windows around closed and he could slink unseen into

Bazza's own garden. But in fact he was not thinking of that, but lying on his belly in the long grass, full of shame and self-loathing.

Then he stood up, shook himself, and jumped through the grass to the fence and buried his muzzle and front paws in the gap beneath it and wriggled back onto his own territory.

I am what I am and there's an end of it.

Bazza sighed and laid his tablet aside. He had found a suitable object, a lady in her thirties, blonde, slightly faded, with large, rather low-slung breasts and large red pointed nipples that stood out against her pale skin. He had worked himself towards a climax, but the cat's terrified cry broke his concentration at quite the wrong moment, with unsatisfactory results. He cleaned himself with a tissue from the dispenser box beside his bed, tucked himself inside his dressing gown and threw the tissue in the toilet before hastening downstairs. If some bloody cat has clawed my dog I'll fucking fricassee it, he told himself, without much thought as to how he would catch the cat in question. He pulled back the old net curtain on the back door, just in time to see the dog wandering slowly across the lawn in the light from the kitchen, apparently

---

unconcerned. The dog stopped, dropped his head and tensed his shoulder muscles, then stretched out his rear legs one after the other and yawned. Bazza opened the door.

"Fuck was that all about then?" he asked. "Sounded like a demon in fucking agony, it did."

Or something that's seen one, thought the dog. He wagged his tail perfunctorily, went to his bowl, lapped a little then curled up in the metal-framed bed near the radiator.

"Good dog," said Bazza.

Oh do fuck off, thought the dog. He rested his muzzle on his paws, tucked his tail below his belly and closed his eyes. Bazza poured himself another amaro and went upstairs.

*

The next day, Bazza and the redhead took the dog for a walk in the park that adjoined the university. The latter was on the edge of the city, and the park surrounded the campus on three sides; it had a lake and woods. It was the cusp of spring and summer, and the afternoon was flooded with gold. Bazza and the redhead walked on ahead together as the dog snuffled through the grass and around the tree-trunks. Now and then Bazza would call "Here boy", and the dog would ignore him, at least at first; then he would look up and see that Bazza and the redhead had got too far ahead, and he would bound along the path until he caught them, though not too fast – he wasn't young. The couple ahead caught halos from the low sun; Bazza's loose wisps of silver hair seemed electric and Caz's red hair shone, and the sun pierced her thin blouse so that you could see her slim waistline through it. From behind her hips swung well and from the front you could clearly see the dark shadow of her nipples through the light material. *Funny, sometimes I think she excites me but then she doesn't and what do you keep, lose and gain of your feelings like that. I get this little frisson but not like when Beryl from Milhamthorpe let me put my hand down her dress when we were 13, and I felt the little mounds get firm under my fingertips and then later she let me feel between the legs and it got all damp and I couldn't control myself and Ma saw my pants and said I was a disgusting boy and I learned to go out and do it in the fields after that. Where are we going? Oh I see, Bazza's making for the landing stage.* He was. They came out of the

23

cool woods and into the sun and then reached the edge of the lake, along which little wooden platforms stuck out into the water, for people to fish or just enjoy the sun. Bazza and Caz sat down facing each other, crosslegged, and closed their eyes. *Oh here we go. I shan't be wanted for a little while then.* The dog lay down in the grass on the bank, on his side, legs stretched out, and enjoyed the gentle warmth of the late afternoon sun. He slept a little, but was woken by Bazza's voice.

"I sort of believe in it," he was saying.

"What, literally? You mean, you won't swat a fly in case it's your reborn grandma?" Caz's voice was low and mellow. The dog found it attractive.

"I don't know about that," said Bazza. "I suppose I'll have to ask Tshering. I thought your soul sort of went back into the pot, part of the life force."

"Well, if it does, you can't attain Nirvana, can you?" said Caz. She took out a cigarette and started to unravel it carefully, then fished in her shoulder bag and bought out a round tin that had once contained sweets. "I mean, you would merge with the rest like a drop of water going into a bath and you wouldn't have an identity that *could* attain Nirvana, yes?"

"Yes," said Bazza. "No. Yes. I don't know. Maybe Tshering can explain everything."

Dad used to take us to church when we were young and then when Cooper sacked him we went less and less and then Ma got that tumour and he were trying to take care of Sis and everything got buggered up and I says one day, we going to church, Dad? and he said, God, what fucking God, no God if you ask me.

"People have always believed in reincarnation," said Caz. "Still do. Alawites and Druzes and people do, don't they?"

"Do they?" asked Bazza. "I wouldn't know. How would they know, anyway? Some bloke comes up to you and says, yeah, lived around here myself a couple of lives ago, tell you what, house prices were lower."

Caz chuckled. She reassembled the cigarette with care. Bazza watched her hands as she did so. Her fingers were very long and her nails were varnished bright green. She lit up, took a few drags and passed it to Bazza.

"People talk about being regressed into past lives, don't they?" she said. "Under hypnosis."

"There was a bloke did that on the TV when I

was in my teens," said Bazza. "Bloxham I think his name was. He regressed this Welshman so he remembered being in Nelson's fleet or something. And someone else claimed she'd been slaughtered in a pogrom in medieval York."

"I didn't know they had pogroms in England," said Caz.

"Yeah, they had pogroms. Anyways, this bloke used to hypnotise them and then record everything on an old reel-to-reel and then they played it back."

Caz frowned. "Funny. I mean, let's say everyone comes back, yes? – and we don't know that. But there are more and more people every year. So where do they get the new souls from? I mean, you could share people across different bodies but they'd sort of get diluted, wouldn't they. And what happens if you're walking down the street and you meet yourself in another body?" She took a deep drag.

"And I wonder what'd make people come back or not come back," said Bazza. "I mean, you're a peasant in rural India or something, you live a really cool life and you help other people dig wells and that, then you die early of hunger, then you come back as a Brahmin or something."

"Yeah, that'll be it won't it," said Caz. She grinned. "And if I live a bad life – let's say I'm a priest and I go round interfering with little boys, or I kill someone, then I come back as a cockroach or an estate agent or something."

"Yeah," said Bazza. He glanced at the dog. "Maybe he did something wicked in a previous life and he's back as a mutt."

The dog howled. He couldn't help it; but he stifled the howl so it only half came out and strangled it into the sort of yelp dogs sometimes let out when they're dreaming. He sat up on his haunches and looked at them.

"Well there you go," said Caz. She reached out to the dog and patted him on the head. "That's who you are, eh? Maybe you organized pogroms in York or something."

The dog submitted to the pats and strokes. He shivered. *Don't think about bad things. Like the vicar who fiddled with the boys at choir practice. Didn't know what it were all about really, if I'd told Dad he'd a been round there with a shotgun. Horrible tweedy wife the vicar had with a booming voice and a mustache. Forget it. Forget it all and you'll feel better. Look at her breasts, that'll do it.* The smoke from the joint made him sneeze. It smelled sweet. He sat in front of Caz as the stroked him and stared straight at the sharp breasts that stood either side of a cleft deepened by the slim leather strap of her bag, emphasizing their firmness; the dark spots of the nipples could be clearly seen. *It's not doing much for me though, is it. That doesn't stay with you.*

A hundred yards or so away a middle-aged woman in a blouse and skirt was walking towards them, a small golden labrador bounding to and from her and wagging its tail. Stupid animal, thought the dog. The labrador ran in a circle and emitted a cheerful little woof, then stopped in front of the woman and wagged its tail. The woman had a thin, severe face and round glasses; her hair was tied back in a single pigtail. "Here Ella!" she called, and took a ball from her shoulder bag and threw it in the direction of the campus. The dog chased it. *Silly animal. Not bad-looking though. Nice glossy coat. And a bitch.* The woman glanced at Bazza and Caz, who were openly passing the joint between them; her face creased with disapproval. The couple either didn't notice or didn't care, the dog was not quite sure which. He watched the labrador bitch. He stood up, stretched, and trotted towards her. The labrador came towards him, wagging her tail, the ball in her mouth. She started to sniff his rear. The dog enjoyed this and sniffed the labrador's. The latter turned away from him and flicked her tail to the side. *Oh no. Don't even think about it. Just go home and lick your balls and stay out of trouble.* The labrador turned her head towards him. She was still holding the ball. *God just like Beryl from Milhamthorpe, she had that swizzle-stick still in her mouth as I felt her up in the bike shed at school, and oh dear, can't help myself, can't stop,* he leapt up on his hind legs and let the front half of his body fall on the labrador's back, grasping her with his front paws, *ooooh that feels very very nice.*

"Get that bloody creature off my Ella!" screamed the woman in a voice of cut glass.

"Oh, hell," said Bazza.

The woman ran towards the dogs, who were about fifty yards from her. She waved her hands in the air; one of them clasped the labrador's lead.

"For God's sake!" she called out. "She's pure-bred!"

"Not the only one," muttered Bazza. More loudly he said: "I really don't think you're supposed to separate them, I think it can hurt them."

Caz snickered.

The woman ignored him and started to flick the lead at the dog.

"Get off her! Get off her, you filthy animal!"

At this point Bazza got up and started towards her in a lumbering half-canter. "Don't you attack my fucking dog like that," he called out. "You'll hurt him."

The lead came down like a whip on the dog's back. Forced to disengage, he yelped with pain and then turned and snarled at the woman, baring his teeth. She drew back; the dog advanced towards her; the labrador gave a little half-yelp, half bark and settled into the grass, letting the ball drop at last.

"Your filthy dog is going to bite me!" she called out. She raised the lead again.

"Come here, boy. Come to Dad," said Bazza.

The dog dropped his head, and turned towards him. He felt Bazza's hand on his neck, gripping him at first, and then the grip turned into a stroke and a pat and felt oddly welcome.

"He's not filthy," Bazza hissed, "and if someone attacked me when I was having sex I'd bloody fight back too."

"Don't you dare speak to me like that! You should've controlled your bloody dog."

"Should've controlled yours," said Bazza. "You have a bitch as a pet, you should bloody well know when it's on heat and keep it away from other dogs."

"Don't you dare speak to me like that!" the woman repeated. She looked at the labrador, who was lying on her belly on the ground, panting and unconcerned. "Poor Ella. And she's a pure-bred too. If she has puppies from this bloody mongrel I shall have to drown the poor things."

The dog broke away from Bazza and snarled, more deeply this time. He crouched down in front of her and seemed for a moment to be about to spring. The woman looked frightened. She backed away.

"You're a disgrace," she said, but her voice quavered a little. "And her." She nodded towards Caz, who was sitting calmly, crosslegged, on the landing stage, smoking the joint, as she had been throughout. "Sitting here smoking drugs in public."

"Who asked you to approve or disapprove of

us," said Bazza. His voice was quiet. *Oh, Bazza, you're angry. Fucking good for you. And I thought you were just a trendy weed-smoking porn-loving student-screwing old fool.* "Come on, dog. Leave her alone. We got better things to do."

"Ella!" called the woman. She bent down and clipped on the lead.

"Fuck's the problem?" Caz called out. She was still sitting on the landing-stage. "Ain't *you* never done it doggy-fashion?"

"Oh! Oh!" The woman drew herself up and turned away.

"Try it!" yelled Caz. "Next time *you're* in heat. You might like it! I do." She swayed from side to side, clasping her knees, laughing.

The dog looked at Ella, who allowed herself to be led away quite happily; she had the ball back in her mouth. *Farewell, my darling,* thought the dog, *and remember: We'll always have Paris.*

He followed Bazza back to the landing stage. Bazza sat down opposite Caz, who reached out and fondled the dog's ears.

"Stupid old cow," said Bazza.

"Hey you," said Caz to the dog. "Good for you. You go for it, boy." She grinned at Bazza. "I bet she *has* done it doggy-fashion. I mean, that way your bloke can't see the fat round your waist and lose his hard-on."

"Ha!" said Bazza. "Nice one." Then he turned to the dog. "But listen, you. Don't you go snarling at strangers, all right, or you'll get us both in trouble." He patted the dog's back. "Not that I blamed you, mate. Wouldn't mind biting her myself." He frowned. "S'funny Caz, he was all right and backing off and then she made that horrid remark about drowning the puppies, and then he went apeshit." He looked at the dog. "S'almost like he understood." He turned to the dog again. "But I mean it, mate. Don't you do that again. 'Cos you know what they do with dogs that attack people, don't you?"

Oh yes, I know. I heard my last owners talk about it after I gave that brat a nip on the arse. Do you reckon he could attack someone, they were saying, should we give him away, should we have him put down. And the man at the sanctuary was nice and said, did the kids tease him, and the man puffs himself up and says no, they never, they're good boys, and I thought, are they fuck. And the sanctuary man said, well, some dogs aren't really good with children, but we don't put them down unless they're dangerous, we just rehome them. Rehome. What a fucking horrible word. Sounds like something out of an engineering manual. "Rehome the inner ring by five and a half thou, ensuring it does not stand proud of the left gurning grommet."

He lay on his side and licked his balls.

"Good lad," said Bazza. "We all got to do that instead sometimes."

*

The station was Victorian and its roof was of curved glass, inspired by Brunel's great wrought-iron spans at Paddington. The sun had come out now, but it had been raining, and the water on the glass above diffused the light so that it settled on the platforms like a shroud. Bazza and Caz stood on the main concourse, their faces strangely flattened by the soft light from above. The dog sat beside them.

He was on the lead. He hated that.

"Does he need to be on the lead?" asked Caz. "I mean, he isn't a stupid dog. Like, he's not going to go chasing the 2.10 to Liverpool Street as it pulls out, is he."

"No, but he might fancy shagging someone's prize Schnauzer and I think I've had enough of that for one week," said Bazza. He yawned. The dog yawned too.

"He's very subdued," said Caz. "Normally he sort of fidgets about, doesn't he, but he's just been sitting there all quiet ever since we came into the station."

"Yeah, funny that," said Bazza. "'Spect he's all right. I love this station, don't you. They've done a brilliant refurb, it's just like it was."

Of course it's not like it was. You don't know. You can't hear the hiss and the clank and what you called a puff but it wasn't a puff, it was a much stronger sound than that, like a thousand bicycle pumps, great clouds of white steam that enveloped you and black smoke that assaulted you with smuts in the eye and the stink of sulphur and the men who leaned out of cabs in their filthy overalls, their faces black with the dust. Last time I came in here, I'd had the letter and, fuck Sergeant Fitch, I thinks, and I goes straight to Captain Parkinson and says, my dad's not doing too well, he's been told to get out of our home, our mum passed away last year, I need to see him. That bastard Fitch was there and says, He should wait for embarkation leave, sir. Parkinson sort of sits there and sucks his teeth for a moment and says, all right, a week's compassionate leave. Bloody furious Fitch was and the next morning he says my kit's out of order and makes me paint coal and makes sure I get kept back for 24 hours. I hope he's rotting in hell.

"Platform 1, look," said Caz, craning her neck to see the board above them – they were standing too close to it. There were a few minutes to go before the London train was due, and the three of them sauntered over to the platform at the left-hand side of the station, past the W.H. Smiths and the off-licence and the entrance to the toilets with their coin-operated barriers. *Never had to spend a penny to spend a penny then.* The flat yellow front of the diesel engine appeared, crossing from track to track at the points before the station so that the train seemed to twist like a snake in the grass.

Bloody horrible journey it was too, waited seven hours for a train and of course it was packed, with everyone's rifle stuck up everyone else's arse and some posh twit of an officer coming down the corridors telling other ranks to let the civilians and orficers have seats, and then the train stops somewhere in Essex and you can hear the odd bomb in the distance and you could just see the searchlights through the blackout curtains. Sat there about an hour. Got in at two in the morning and walked seven miles to

---

Milhamthorpe and then this bloke picks me up in an RAF fuel bowser and he's smoking, bloody idiot, lucky we didn't go sky-high, not surprised we were losing the bloody war. Oh, here he is. What fetching robes.

The monk descended from the front most carriage. He was tall and muscular and his face was dominated by his high cheekbones; his head was shaved and he wore reddish-orange robes and, oddly somehow, trainers.

"He looks as if he could beat someone to a pulp," said Bazza.

"That wouldn't be very karmic, Bazza," said Caz.

The monk approached, set down his modest case and bowed.

"Tshering," he said in a voice that seemed too high for his large body.

"Barry," said Bazza, "but Bazza will do. This is Caroline but everyone calls her Caz."

"Indeed," said the monk. He inclined his head a little. "Tshering is, in fact, my only name. But I am called Tshering Thinley for passport purposes. It seems one cannot cross borders with just one name; though I have never felt I needed more."

He looked down at the dog.

"And this is the dog," explained Caz.

Tshering made as if to pat him, then hesitated. He looked into the dog's eyes. The dog looked back. They stared at each other for several seconds. The dog put his head slightly on one side. Tshering did the same. He frowned. He muttered something.

"I'm sorry?" said Caz.

"I beg your pardon, I spoke in Dzongkha," said Tshering.

"You're all right with dogs?" said Bazza anxiously.

"Oh yes," said Tshering. "My father was a yak-herder. We had many dogs to protect the yak. Bears and boar are a problem, you see, especially in winter pasture."

"Oh," said Bazza. "They must be big dogs if they fight bears."

"They are *very* big dogs," said Tshering, smiling. Then his face grew serious again as he looked at the dog. Now he did bend down and pat the animal gently on the neck.

"Sometimes," said Caz, "we think he is an old soul."

Tshering chuckled. He seemed to relax as they left the station. "We do not think in such a way," he said. "To be sure, when one passes, one's spirituality may enter another realm, but not one's spirit; there is no individual – one is – what did your Milton say? – each one a part of the main."

"You have read Milton?" asked Caz.

"You are surprised?" said Tshering. He smiled. "But you know, when we were in winter pasture, my parents would send me to an aunt in a village below, where I could go to school; and I had an Indian teacher, from Cochin, who read it to us. He wanted us to understand that Buddhism was more complicated than we thought. Until then, all I knew of religion was the terrifying deities on the temple walls, and the phallic paintings on the houses in the valleys."

He thought for a moment, then intoned:

No man is an island,
Entire of itself,
Every man is a piece of the continent,
A part of the main.
If a clod be washed away by the sea,
Europe is the less.

"You remember it," said Bazza, impressed.

"I searched for it later. I did not stay at school. I was the middle child, and when I was about eight, my parents gave me to a monastery so that they might acquire merit," said Tshering.

Wonder if Dad ever acquired any merit. God knows he tried hard enough. That last visit, it was early winter and the fuel bowser dropped me off at the end of the track to the cottage, just after dawn. "I'd take you down mate, but if I get stuck the sergeant will pull my knackers off," he said. Your sergeant; you should meet mine, I thought. It was about a mile and a half to the cottage. It had rained heavily in the night. The sky was a dirty grey, with wisps of darker black lower down, but there was plenty of light to catch the puddles between the wheel-ruts that cut through the caramel earth. The fields were bare – nothing in fallow, the Ministry wasn't having that, make 'em grow something on every damn inch. Old Cooper was growing winter vegetables. He always had of course. We used to eat turnip tops for greens. I never liked them. The track had never been fenced, but now it was, against thieving, and barbed wire stretched along either side. One stretch was lined with the black carcasses of crows. A light-brown and grey-green world, spotted with black. Soon my boots were splattered with mud and I wondered how I'd clean them on the way back to camp. It didn't matter. That pig Fitch would've put me on a charge anyway. The bright grey light hurt my eyes. The dog closed his eyes, and opened them; it was a bright Saturday afternoon in early summer and they were across the river from the station and walking along the towpath, a cloud of chatter drifting towards them from the riverside pub where away fans gathered before City games, most just happy, but some flushed and roaring; a few policemen and women were standing on the bridge. Tshering's robes had drawn an ironic cheer as they walked past. Someone muttered something about slitty eyes. But if Tshering heard he affected not to, and they drew away and passed under an aisle of willows, the river on their right; to their left was a meadow scattered with boys in whites, and now and then there was the crack of leather on willow and sudden animation as someone tried for a run or ran for the ball. Beyond the meadow the spire of the cathedral reached for a pale-blue sky scattered with bright white clouds. There were no crows.

*

Bazza's sister, Destiny, did bring Clarissa by early in the week, as she had said she would. With them was Destiny's second husband, a small man who worked in human resources and who asked Bazza if he could watch the cricket. For Bazza, who found both cricket and human resources turgid, this was satisfactory. Clarissa was 11 and rather small and wore a light floral-print dress. Destiny was 50, broad-shouldered, wore a skirt and brogues and was vaguely hairy. Bazza escorted the pair into the garden, where Caz was sitting on a canvas barbecue chair, her knees drawn up in front of her, her bare feet hanging over the edge of the canvas seat so that her bright-green nail-varnish was clearly on view. She wore the same light cotton blouse but had heard about Destiny so had put on a bra and had nipped out the large spliff she had been smoking when the doorbell rang, and had concealed it in her shoulder-bag.

"This is Caz," said Bazza.

"Indeed," said Destiny, glancing briefly at Caz and turning towards the canvas seats that leaned folded against the kitchen wall. "Shall we sit down?"

"Of course," said Bazza. He made to unfold

one of the seats but his sister immediately took it from him and started to do so herself, so he grasped the other one. When they were set up, they sat down. Clarissa remained standing, looking around the garden. She was pale with reddish-brown hair and a hint of freckles.

"Clarissa should have brought her sun-hat," said Destiny. "Or John should have remembered."

A distant roar arose from the television in the front room. Another English batsman had fallen to an Australian fast bowler.

"I think I left a Panama hat upstairs," said Caz.

Destiny ignored this.

"Would you like something to drink?" asked Bazza.

"Tea," said Destiny. "And for John. I suppose there is no barley water for Clarissa?"

"I got some Coke and Sprite for her," said Bazza.

"They are full of sugar and quite unsuitable," said Destiny.

Clarissa remained standing, still looking around the garden in a vague, unfocused way.

"Clarissa, would you like to meet Uncle

Bazza's new pet?" said Caz. "We got a dog."

"I heard you had got a dog," said Destiny, addressing Bazza rather than Caz. "I didn't hear any barking."

"He doesn't bark much," said Bazza. "He's funny like that. Doesn't seem very interested in humans. We can pet him, but he's not affectionate. I think he had some trouble with children in his last family."

"We had better keep him away from Clarissa then," said Destiny. "Where is this wretched animal?"

Bazza pointed down the garden to the rhododendron bushes. "There he is. He likes to slob out in the shade when it's warm."

"Clarissa, what would you like to drink?" asked Caz.

The girl was still standing immobile and staring down the garden. "She can't hear a word you're saying," said Destiny, but Caz was already standing. She moved round in front of the girl and smiled. The girl started a little, but then smiled back. She had grey eyes that sparkled and dimples at the corners of her mouth.

"Hello," she said.

"Hello," said Caz. "Can you lipread?" She spoke quite slowly.

"Sometimes," she said. "Depends." Her pronunciation was a little unusual and Caz realised she had probably never heard other people's voices normally.

The dog, sensing movement, stirred; he had been lying on his side beneath a bush, but now he rolled onto his belly and looked back up the garden to the house. Like many in that Edwardian suburb, the garden was narrow but unusually long. The dog saw Caz stand in front of the girl and smile, speak a few words, then raise her hands to her shoulder. "My name is Caz," she said slowly, and as she did so she started to move her hands. The girl answered with similar movements.

"Good Lord," said Destiny. "How would this woman know British Sign Language?"

Caz turned to her, and said briefly, "My brother is profoundly deaf." Then she turned back to Clarissa. "Would you like something to drink? What would you like?"

"Coke please," said Clarissa.

"Clarissa, that is terrible for your teeth," said Destiny.

"She can't hear a word you're saying," said Caz.

"*Well!*" said Destiny.

At that moment they were interrupted. The dog came half-trotting, half-running down the garden, his tail waving from side to side. When he reached Clarissa and Caz he sat down in front of the former and looked up at her. He wagged his tail, and because he was sitting, it swept back and forth across the grass. He licked his lips and gave a little whine.

"Oh lovely," said Clarissa. She knelt down and reached out towards the dog. He stood, his tail, in fact his whole rear end, wagging enthusiastically; and put his head into her lap. She leant over and hugged him.

"For Heaven's sake, Clarissa, it's a *dog*," said Destiny.

"I do believe you're right," said Bazza. Then he frowned, and looked at Caz. "He's never done anything like that before, has he? He doesn't mind people but mostly he just ignores them."

"I would like a dog," said Clarissa.

"Clarissa, for Heaven's sake get away from that animal," said Destiny, but she seemed to say it to herself, aware that Clarissa would not understand unless facing her. The dog looked up at Clarissa's face and she looked down at his.

"I'll make the tea," said Bazza.

He went into the kitchen. As he did so Tshering emerged into the garden, robes flowing.

"Good Lord," said Destiny.

The kitchen window opened.

"This is Tshering, who is staying with me for a few weeks," said Bazza.

"I see," said Destiny. She stood up doubtfully and held out her hand. Tshering grasped it warmly in both of his.

"*Kuzuzampo-la,*" he said.

"I beg your pardon?"

"It is the greeting in my language, Dzongkha," said Tshering. "It means, literally, 'How's your body?'"

Bazza chuckled. "You do not ask, 'How's your soul?' when you meet people?"

"I do not feel that is necessary in this instance," said Tshering, looking into Destiny's eyes. She looked a little uncomfortable and disengaged her hand.

"Very nice to meet you," she said.

Caz emerged with a pint glass and a two-litre bottle of Coke. She gave it to Clarissa.

"She really should not be drinking that dreadful stuff," said Clarissa, who appeared glad of a distraction. "It's not just bad for the teeth. So many of my patients come into surgery overweight. The rise in type 2 diabetes is quite shocking."

"I expect you tell them the error of their ways," said Caz.

Destiny ignored this. She turned her attention to her brother. "You haven't said recently what's happening with Ellen. Have you seen her?"

"No, happily," said Bazza. "Not that I've tried."

"Really, Barnabas, I wish you would make *some* effort to get back together with her," said Destiny.

"Barnabas? *Barnabas*? Is that really your real name?" said Caz. "How lovely." She grinned.

Bazza came out into the garden with his sister's tea. He had gone a little red.

"Well, yes, but most people called me Barney when I was little," he said.

"What, you mean like that crappy bright-purple dinosaur that goes round spreading peace and love?" said Caz. "Actually the description suits you quite well, apart from being purple, though sometimes your face is after you've been on top, of course."

Destiny's face was a thunderbolt.

"The dog appears to be laughing," said Tshering quietly.

It was true. The dog's mouth was open and his tongue was hanging out.

"Don't *you* start," said Bazza.

The dog quickly disguised the laugh as a pant. He put his head back in Clarissa's lap and she fondled his ears.

"I'm not getting back with her, Dest," said Bazza. He wasn't smiling. "Sorry. I know you liked her. I just got fed up with being approved or disapproved of all the time, I suppose. People do, you see."

Yep, dogs feel much the same way.

Destiny's face was no longer like thunder. She looked upset.

"Drink your tea, it'll get cold," said Bazza. "Have we got any biccies, Caz? Did we finish the chocolate Digestives?"

"No, we got some. I'll get them," said Caz, and suddenly she sounded a little subdued too.

Destiny went not long afterwards. They all trooped through the house, Destiny in the lead,

Bazza next, Clarissa and the dog following him and Caz bringing up the rear.

Destiny stuck her head inside the living room.

"Time to go, dear, there's that stew in the Crock-Pot," she boomed.

John was small and had nasal hair. He was staring at the television, transfixed.

"He's on *87 not out*!" he said.

"Yes, dear," said Destiny. Her husband stood up; he came to just over Caz's chest height and found himself staring at her blouse, through which her black bra showed clearly. His jaw dropped a little further. He was shooed out to the compact Audi that stood in the street and sat in the front passenger seat, sighing deeply.

Clarissa turned, knelt down and gave the dog a hug. Then she got in the car. The dog gave a little whimper. As the car pulled away he stood, wagging his tail uncertainly, watching her wave to him across the parcel shelf.

In the garden, Tshering remained in his chair. He was perfectly still, and remained so as Bazza and Caz came back into the garden. They sat down and stayed silent themselves.

After a moment Tshering spoke.

"The path through samsara is long," he said,

"and to ease it one should think in generous ways. That is the energy that guides the path and lifts a being to the higher realms; from the animal state to the human world, in which one has freedom of decision and may acquire merit."

"I thought that one should abandon the concept of the self?" said Bazza, looking up. He was rolling a joint.

"Yes," said Tshering, "but also one must emit positive energy; one must feed one's karma, which may be considered a mental state. One may do this, at least in part, through compassion to all sentient beings."

Bazza nodded.

"She is not so bad," he said, almost to himself. "She loves Clarissa and has poured endless time and energy into her, into helping her lipread, learn sign-language, learn to speak."

"Indeed," said Tshering. "But do not say that. Feel it. That is the way of the dharma."

"And the practice – no, the feeling – of compassion will bring us happiness and peace?" said Caz.

"Yes," said Tshering. "But beer also helps."

"There's a six-pack in the fridge," said Caz.

"I know," said Tshering. "I obtained it earlier.

I was not sure which beer was of the highest class, so I purchased one named – what is it? – Special Brew. I hope that is appropriate."

The sun was lower now but shone straight on them, as the back of the house faced west. Tshering and Bazza sat with cans of beer, watching the shadows lengthen, and their faces were suffused with yellow-golden light. "It's so beautiful," said Caz. She slipped into the house and emerged a moment later with her iPhone and Bazza's selfie stick.

"Family portrait," she announced.

"Oh," said Bazza. "Let's kneel on the grass. It'll be easier to get us all in."

He and Tshering knelt close together and Caz knelt a little higher behind them.

"The dog," she said. "I mean, we can't leave the dog out."

"Oh right," said Bazza. He clicked his tongue loudly. "Dog! Come!"

Oh, fuck off, Barnabas. It isn't suppertime yet. Go and spread some peace and love, you hippy dinosaur.

He opened his eyes. The three of them were there at the end of the garden, in a neat little triangle.

"Family portrait, dog," called Caz. "Can't

have it without you."

Oh, well, put like that...

He stood, stretched and ambled slowly down the garden. Bazza patted the grass in front of them, and the dog sat down, his tongue hanging out. Then Bazza took the selfie stick and Caz put her arms round the shoulders of both men, and Bazza snapped them two, three, four times, grinning, and then Caz stuck her tongue out, and the dog stuck his out at the same time, and when they saw the picture they roared with laughter and Caz pressed share and put it on Facebook straightaway, tagging Bazza and Tshering, and the dog through the page Bazza had set up for him, and Tshering through his public page *The Practice of the Dharma*. Tshering saw it the next morning and was about to hide the post from his timeline. Then he looked at the four faces, the three human ones glowing from the sunset and from pleasure and warmth and compassion for sentient beings. He clicked *Like* instead.

*

Caz stayed that night and they went to bed early, Bazza asking Tshering if he might "let the dog out" before he went to bed. Tshering politely agreed. It was only ten, so he went through to the living room, where Bazza had thoughtfully retuned the TV to BBC Four. "They have some excellent documentaries and arts programmes," he explained. Tshering thanked him and waited until he heard the toilet flush a second time upstairs, then decided he would not be disturbed. He retuned the TV to Sky Sports. "All right, my friend," he said to the dog, "I will let you out. Jump at the door when you want to be let back in."

He looked at the dog in a speculative fashion. The dog cocked his head on one side and looked back.

"What was your realm?" asked Tshering. "But that is a silly question, because you cannot tell me, can you?"

He smiled and stroked the dog on the back.

"All right, go and do what you have to do," he said. "And remember, if you meet a cat, to have compassion for other sentient beings. Also it may scratch your eye out."

He took a beer from the fridge and then looked back down the garden, frowning. The dog disappeared behind the rhododendron bushes.

Tshering returned to the TV, which was showing highlights of a pre-season friendly between City and Dynamo Kyiv. He sat back, took a draught of beer, belched and felt a gentle weight on his eyelids. Clarissa and Destiny crossed his mind and he smiled, and let a mental mantra run quietly in their name.

The dog slipped below the rhododendron bushes. He was hidden here, but not comfortable; there was little space below the boughs, and he wanted to stretch, to lie, to rest his heavy limbs. He relieved himself briefly, then pushed his haunches through the shallow gap beneath the fence and into the neighbour's garden. He could have pressed on through the next fence and onto Richard's bleak patio. Instead he lay down in the long grass, snorting slightly as some seed or other touched his nostrils.

He thought of Clarissa and the touch of her hand as she fondled his ears and the texture of her soft, simple cotton shift. *Dad didn't ought of let Sis go really. Sitting there shaking his head. Don't know what else I could have done, son. Well I didn't know what to say to that, I'd just been to see her. When I went off to the army the first time it was*

summer and she gave me a good smile and a goodbye
hug and when Mum sent her last letter there were
pressed flowers from Sis in the envelope. So I go to the
County place and it's a big old house from the last
century, built for some rich chap who'd fallen on hard
times, or maybe just wanted somewhere less draughty.
The bus dropped me at the gate and I walked the
quarter-mile up the drive to the house. Big red-brick
place with white wood trimmings round the eaves, tall
windows, and the windows had bars on them. There's
this porter on the desk with a wheeze and a cough and
a military way of holding himself. You been gassed
just like Dad, I think. Wait here, son, he says, I'll ask
Sister Patrick, and he goes up the stairs and I hear
voices and then this woman saying, oh yes, I know the
one, Nurse Smithers caught her interfering with
herself in the night, the filthy girl. He an officer? And
the porter chap says, no, he's a private, ma'am. Then
he can make an appointment and come back, she says.
And the porter says, well, he's on leave I suppose, and
maybe he didn't have a telephone. He comes down a
few minutes later with a young nurse with a thin pale
spotty face. Sister Patrick says as you're to come with
me, she says, not a trace of a smile, and I follow her up
the stairs with my cap in my hand, all lino, clean as a
whistle, stinking of disinfectant. She's in a ward, just

iron beds, and iron bars on the window, and she doesn't hear our footsteps coming of course, and she's sitting on her bed like the others and when she turns round she catches sight of me; her face seems completely vacant, and then she sees it's me and she stands up and she's shaking and I hug her and we sit for a while but she doesn't try to speak, as she used to; and after twenty minutes the rat-faced nurse comes back and wants me to go and I won't and the sister comes and finally the old porter comes up and he's wheezing from the stairs and, time to go son, he says, and I do then, because he's been gassed like Dad; and I hug Sis again and when I turn back at the door she's just standing there with tears streaming down her face and I go out and wait in the rain and there's no bus and then a big Humber stops and I get ready to get in but it's an orrrficer and the lump of shit wants to know why my cap badge isn't straight. But then the coal lorry comes by and they sit me in the cab between them and I get home and it's still raining and the afternoon is fading and the room is filled with thin grey light. You seen her then, says Dad and he's sitting there all upright and rigid with his hands on the arms of the chair and his feet together and he's not looking at me. I'm sorry son, don't know what else I could've done, he says again. Not got your ma around

---

to help any more, and now I got the heave-ho from Coopers I can't stay here, so where'm I to put her, I'm going to your gran and she's barely got room for me. We sit there a long time, the light fading, just a little heat coming off the range, just enough to keep us from shivering all the time.

When you coming next, he asks in the end. Don't know Dad, this was embarkation leave. Don't know where we're going but that bastard Fitch says it's India. Don't you fucking go there, says Dad. Your uncle Don was there. Other ranks get treated like dirt in India. You'll spend six days a week square-bashing and on Sunday it's church parade then nothing, and you'll be there for years. Least the Germans aren't in India yet though, I says. Shan't have to fight.

Don't be too sure, he says, they have riots and all that. They'll make you kill those black people. Why you want to hurt the likes of them, God only knows. God knows what the empire ever did for the likes of us. Your grandad, he walks away in a nice red coat one summer's day and never comes back. Killed by the Boers. What was all that for then?

He's still not looking at me. He gets up, puts a bit more slag into the range, then sits down heavily, coughs a bit, then says:

Don't you go to India, son. Scarper.

They'd get me, Dad.

They got you anyway. Get out of here in the morning, before your leave's up. This is the first place they'll look.

I'm due back in camp on Sunday night. The next day is Friday. I think about things in the night, listening to my Dad coughing in the other room. I think of Sis crying and that swine officer in the rain and Fitch who puts me on jankers most days and made me paint coal. In the morning my Dad makes me some tea and bread and dripping, all there is in the house. I shan't see him again. Or Sis. He'll be dead now of course, and Sis too, well she'd be over ninety. 'Course, I never saw her no more neither. Dad and I, we didn't hug or anything, we weren't like that really, we just nod at each other and I take my rifle and pack. It's not raining now, the clouds are high and thin and they've drawn back a bit so there's a pale-blue winter sky; and this time I don't look back, just walk steadily along the rutted, puddly brown track, past the crows.

The grass tickled the dog's snout again and he sneezed. He opened his eyes. The warmth of the night chased his thoughts away; spring was really turning to summer now, and the air was soft and aromatic and the moon, nearly full, shot the garden full of silver. The dog caught a familiar scent. He stood stock-still for a moment, trying to trace it, then became aware of a movement near him and raised his muzzle, which had been resting, as was his habit, on his crossed paws. He tensed. The big old cat was looking at him from two or three yards away, through a gap in the grass made by the path to the garden shed. It hissed, and then leaned back; but it did not yowl or flee. It seemed to study the dog, eye to eye. *Something has changed*, it seemed to say. Then it turned and slipped away to the wall, mounted it, turned and looked back at the dog, almost with interest; and then it was gone, into Richard's arid garden next door.

The dog looked after it for a moment; then he stood, stretched as usual, and picked his way through the long grass to the hole below the fence, and slithered through it into the space behind the rhododendron bush. He came out from the narrow gap between the bushes and onto the lawn, bending his body like a weasel or a stoat. The light from the open kitchen door caught his eyes, which seemed to glitter in the semi-darkness. Tshering sat on the step, his robes rucked up so that the chunky black trainers he wore were clearly visible beneath. He had a can in his hand. As he watched the dog approach, he pulled the ring-pull on the can, then took the dog's own bowl and set it on the ground beside him. He poured a little beer into the bowl. The dog came slowly up to the bowl, stuck his tongue in the beer and lapped, slowly at first then faster and faster as he remembered the ancient taste, his head twisting this way and that.

When it was finished, he looked up at the monk, licked his chops and gave a little belch. He cocked his head on one side and gave a tentative wag of the tail.

"I thought you were very nice with that young girl this afternoon," said Tshering. He took a swig of beer from the can. "You acquired merit, so now you should have a little beer."

He patted the ground beside him with his hand and the dog sat down beside him, facing the same way towards the bushes at the end of the garden. Tshering put his hand on the dog's haunches and gave them a little squeeze.

"My brothers used to give the dogs *bangchang* sometimes, if they had chased off a bear, or a wild boar," he said. "It was a prank. My father did not like it. But the dogs did."

The dog looked sideways at the monk and

grinned. Well, sort of opened his mouth and let his tongue hang out to one side.

"We lived in a black yak-hair tent," said the monk. "High in the mountains. Even the winter pasture was at three thousand meters. The dogs slept outside. Once, an Indian forester stayed with us for the night. He thought to attract a dog's attention – I do not remember why; and he whistled." He looked at the dog. "In our country you must not whistle after dark. It will alert spirits, even demons, to your presence. My father was very frightened. The next day one of our dogs was gored by a boar."

He took another draught of beer, then held the can in front of him, his free hand still on the dog's haunches.

"It was a coincidence, of course," he said.

They both looked at the moon.

"Sometimes I wonder what the people here really expect of me," said Tshering. "They think I have a spirituality that is higher than their own. In fact, sometimes I think that all I have is knowledge of my ignorance. But perhaps that is itself the spirituality that they seek."

He looked at the dog again. The dog looked back. Then – it did not know why – it stood, and licked Tshering on the ear. The monk was momentarily startled; then he laughed, and hugged the dog. Then he pulled back, still with his hands on the dog's back, and looked it in the eye.

"It is a long journey," he said. "We do not remember our former realms. People tried. The Buddha counselled them to refrain. No good, he said, would come of it. The past realm is not important. What matters is this one, and the next."

He took a final mouthful of beer, and shook the can to see if it was empty; it was.

"Now we shall rest," he said. The dog followed him through the kitchen door, and Tshering locked and bolted it firmly for the night; no bear, boar or burglar would disturb them.

*

The next day Caz gave the dog a bath.

"You can't do that," said Bazza. "He'll go batshit."

"Well, he does pong a little," said Caz. "I don't care, but with Richard and Wendy coming round tonight – and anyway, he had a shag the other day."

"So?"

"Well, even you have a shower after a shag, don't you?" she said. "Mind you, the dog's got more class than you, Barnabas dear."

"Have it your own way then," said Bazza. "But if he bites your fingers off, don't say I didn't warn you."

The dog didn't bite but he was reluctant to climb the stairs; he wasn't allowed up there, and two or three times he stopped and looked up at Caz, who was kneeling at the top.

"Come on, it's all right, you're going to have a lovely bath," she said.

We never had those, not that way. There was a tin tub Ma used to drag in front of the fire in winter and in the summer sometimes she'd bathe us outside, but either way the water got cold quickly. Dad used to whiff a bit when he'd been with the cattle. Suppose we didn't mind that much, not really. Long as we were all warm in the evenings, and we were after Mrs Berry died and we got her coal, that was lovely, for about three months that one winter, must have been about two or three years before the war. That was when Prince used to curl up in front of the fire and make little grunting sounds when he was dreaming. 'Spose he were dreaming of something nice, not like I do; rabbits maybe – he used to give a little whimper of excitement sometimes – not like me when I wake up whining and howling. Still, we know why that is, don't we.

"In the bath with you," said Caz, lifting the dog over the edge and setting him down ever so gently at the shallow end of the bath. "Let's have you sitting there while I get the water right so it feels nice." She turned the hot and cold taps and ran her hand through the water for a moment or two, then lifted the shower head off its mountings. "You're going to love this, dog. And I'm going to let you have some of Bazza's tea tree shampoo. Wasted on him, really, he's got a lot less hair than you have. Now, feel the water." And she lifted the dog's paw and aimed the shower at it. "Feels nice does it?"

Does rather. Ooh that's very nice. Well aren't I a lucky dog. First I get beer, then I get a nice hot shower. Ain't you got any ass's milk, Miss?

The dog closed his eyes and leaned forward as the warm water cascaded over his back. He didn't protest. To Caz's surprise he thumped his tail against the enamel. She worked the shampoo gently into his coat, little by little so that she did not use more than she really needed, and then washed it out quickly and thoroughly. She turned off the tap and put the shower attachment back in its cradle.

"Now you're gonna shake the water off all over me, aren't you, you little sod," she said.

I do believe I am. Stand back, madam.

"Whoaaa!" She was kneeling on the bathroom floor; hands on knees, she threw her head back and laughed as the water made a hundred spots on her white blouse and started to join up so that the blouse became, in places, transparent. "I'll tell you what we'll do, dog. At the next County Show we'll have a combined dog show and Wet Tee-Shirt compo. All right? Now, keep still as I rub you down." And she got Bazza's towel and firmly but gently dried the dog as best she could. He stood there with his tongue hanging out.

"All right, come down into the sunshine and I'll finish the job," she said, and she took a cordless hairdryer that was resting on the linen bin and hopped downstairs two at a time, the dog in pursuit. They went into the garden, where Bazza and Tshering were sitting in deck chairs with mugs of tea.

"Now, sit. Good dog." She pointed the hairdryer away from the dog and switched it on, in the Hot setting, and put her hand in front of it to test the temperature. She turned it down. "That'll be all OK," she said. "Right, keep still, dog. Treat coming." And she started to blow-dry his hair, combing it out slowly and carefully so as not to pull on the knots in the fur.

The dog wagged his tail across the grass.

"He's got a nice coat, really, hasn't he," said Bazza.

"Oh yes," said Caz. "It's a bit border collie, isn't it, with the long hair on the chest and the white boots and ruff. His muzzle's sort of border-shaped as well. I wonder if he's a sheepdog really." She switched off the dryer, leaned forward and gave the dog a little hug around the neck, and felt his nose against her ear.

"We never gave him a proper name really," said Bazza.

"You shoulda done that," said Caz.

"I know," said Bazza. "But I sort of thought, well, he's been around for a while, and I reckon he's been given at least one name already. Don't want to tell him what his name is. Sort of disrespectful."

Bazza, you're not a complete dick after all, are you. Not sure I can deal with this.

"Well, let's think of some nice names," said Caz. "And then we can say them to him and see if he looks impressed."

There's a sort of black feeling rising up inside me because you don't know and you don't see what I am and you couldn't understand what I am and you don't understand that I'm damned, I'm cursed, I'm fucking scum, and you can't love me and you can't stroke me like this.

The dog stood and wriggled out of Caz's arms and walked slowly towards the rhododendron bushes.

"Oh dear, I wonder what we said," said Caz.

"Dunno," said Bazza. "He's funny, that dog is. I've had him a month and he's never liked people. Never hurt anyone, mind. Just doesn't give a shit. And now he's sort of showing affection and then not and then licking your ear and then getting snotty again. Funny, I gone out with a couple of women like that. But that was their monthly sometimes."

"Barnabas," said Caz, "you are a sexist fucking pig. If you didn't eat pussy like a gourmet I'd wring your fucking neck."

Tshering had been dozing in his deckchair. He opened his eyes slowly.

"Oh, God, I'm so sorry, Tshering," said Caz, her hand flying to her mouth.

Tshering rubbed his eyes.

"Don't worry," he said. "But a pussy is a sentient being, and like dogs, they are worthy of respect. I do not believe you should eat them."

"She didn't mean – well, in this country we don't – yes, well," said Bazza, grimacing with embarrassment.

"They eat horses in some places," said Caz.

Tshering closed his eyes again. Caz noticed a smile playing around the corners of his mouth; he was clearly trying to suppress it.

"You were talking about the dog," he said quietly.

"He's a strange one," said Bazza.

Tshering opened his eyes again. The dog was lying under one of the rhododendron bushes at the end of the garden. His front legs were parallel, a little apart; his rear legs were curled together on one side, and he was looking back down the garden at them, his tongue hanging out. Tshering looked back. The dog lowered his eyes, licked his teeth, and closed his muzzle then lowered it onto the ground between his forepaws.

Tshering stood. He walked slowly down the garden. The dog watched him come, his red and orange robes swirling around the trainers below them. For a moment the monk stood above him, looking down. Then he drew his habit up to his knees and sat down beside the dog, clasping his knees, on which he rested his chin; he was not looking at the dog.

At the other end of the garden, Bazza leaned back in his deckchair.

"What time are Richard and Wendy coming?" she said.

"Not till seven," said Bazza.

"Skin up then?"

"Go on," said Bazza. "Then I'll do the dhal for later. Maybe you can do the rice when they come. I'm crap at that."

Tshering looked toward them. He saw Caz take her tin and her papers from her shoulder-bag. He turned to the dog.

"I love rhododendrons," he said. "I wonder what these look like at their best. But they are young bushes, aren't they? There is little to see as yet."

The dog did not reply.

"I miss them so much," said Tshering. "In my country they appear in April, like red and yellow fire. In the valley they die soon, but they move up the mountain. By the end of May they are long gone. But then you can walk up through the forests of the Talakha range, and on the summit you will still find them."

He fell silent for a moment, and thought of the rhododendrons; not long into spring they would be long gone in the valley. But at 3,500 metres they were glorious in late May and into June. You walked through forests of cool damp moss and through fronds of Spanish fern; and then you saw them, near the summit, bright against the blue and white sky that foreshadowed the coming of the north-east monsoon.

"The way from realm to realm is hard," he said.

The dog looked at him.

"When we climb our mountains," said Tshering, "sometimes we take twigs or leaves from the ground, and carry them with us as we go higher. Then we leave them on an upper slope, maybe in a cairn of stones. We like to help nature. We like to help it climb higher, to take it to new places, so the life force spreads and grows."

He thought for a moment.

"Sometimes I am homesick," he said.

The dog sat up and continued to look at him, head slightly askew.

"The way is hard," repeated Tshering.

He stroked the dog on the back, then sighed and stood. He went back towards the house.

There is no way, you idiot. I'm just damned. Don't you understand that? I already knew it that night itself; it was the woman in the dark-blue suit who made me understood that, made me see that we were all damned, but I must have known it by then, somewhere in the corners of my mind. I can see her quite clearly.

Most of the people who came were men, about half in uniform, but many civilians, sometimes suited in the tired cloth of the time, sometimes in dungarees or overalls, the latter brown from the stores or white and streaked with dirt, from Smithfield or Billingsgate; sometimes they smelt of offal or fish. But usually it was small men in shabby suits with raincoats and bowlers or trilbies on their knees, leaning towards the ring under the harsh light from the naked lightbulbs and mouthing Kill him! Kill him! *That night Clyde* _nearly did, his final blow sending a beefy Guardsman across the ring and into the ropes, and there was stamping and cheering from many of the audience. I sat there and didn't care, because the odds were always short on Clyde, and we never lost more than a shilling or a florin a head. We could well afford the three or four pounds we'd pay the losing fighters, and they'd earned it. Once or twice there were men who could have killed Clyde if it'd been a straight fight. He was huge, and had the strength of three men, but he was slow, slow from the booze and the blows he'd took in the days when he fought for real. But when he hit a man, he hit hard. Too many patsies we had that said yes thirty bob and I'll throw the fight and they never thought it would be real like that, that they'd pay for their thirty bob with blows that rained down on them from the crown to the groin, because Clyde didn't like white men. I tried to be friendly once or twice, at first; but it was a mistake. It was an innocent question. Would he go back to Mississippi one day, I asked him. No, he says, I'm not gonna swing from a branch like my brother did when they found he'd had a white woman; and the hatred blazed in his eyes. I knew to leave Clyde alone after that. He wouldn't hurt me. He depended on me, and I on him, and all of us on each other, living on our wits, no love or trust, no_ comradeship, just the fear shared by the damned.

I knew the face of the woman in the blue suit. I couldn't place it but I knew it. It came to me the third or fourth time she turned up, the wife of an MP, once a successful barrister, now serving in the regiment from which I'd deserted. He was lately missing in Malaya. There'd been a picture of her in the London Evening News, *clutching her purse, in a little hat with a veil, looking suitably grief-stricken. I didn't think his loss troubled her. She had fine features of porcelain, her eyes dark, her skin delicate and pale, but it flushed as she watched the fight, and her mouth was a wide slack slash that was out of place in that delicate face and as Clyde pummelled the guardsmen and the crowd roared and the cigarette-smoke gathered below the naked lights, I looked from her to the ring and back again.*

A gout of blood came from the Guardsman's mouth and I realised that he was trying to attract George's attention to stop the fight, but George moved around the ring, avoiding the flailing bodies, with a bow tie as if this was a proper match, not a dog-fight in an abandoned cellar below a bombsite. His white shirt was spotted with blood. The Guardsman wanted to concede. Clyde wanted to kill him. The crowd was roaring. I looked at the woman. She was watching intently, sitting very erect, her torso moving slowly, rhythmically, and now and then the sound of a sharp blow made her eyes close briefly and then her hand moved across her front and her fingers seemed to be reaching down between her legs, and I watched her with both revulsion and arousal. Dragging my eyes away I suddenly saw George dragging Clyde off the Guardsman, who was lying in the ring, blood pouring from his nose and mouth, his face a mass of weals. "Fair fight!" someone yelled. "Time to get off him!" And there were grunts of agreement as the cheers died down. George helped the guardsman out of the ring and into the storeroom at the back. The woman in the blue suit stayed seated as the audience filed out. I opened the box and paid out the winnings, such as they were. I could hear Briscoe at the door, telling people to mind the blackout curtain. Briscoe was a rat-faced little man who hadn't actually deserted; he was stationed not far away and his specialty was tyres and other parts, but he'd got me my new uniform, 2nd Lt., Ox & Bucks Light Infantry, very nice, and my revolver as well.

The last men had filed out when the woman stood and came to me. I had been watching her from the corner of my eye, though I was busy, calculating the takings. Briscoe would get £4 14s 6d, more than the

***

little shit deserved, to my mind. I'd pocket £6 6s 2d. Clyde would get the lion's share, nearly £15. I wondered what he would do with it all. The other hangers-on would get a quid or so each and we'd stand the Guardsman a fiver. I straightened a small tower of florins and looked towards the improvised ring. The woman was walking towards me; she still wore the hat but without the veil, and her thick chestnut hair had come unpinned and was straggling from below the brim. The top button of her blouse was undone. In the harsh light from the naked bulb I could see that she was older than I'd thought, but still not more than thirty-five. There were a few lines around the dark, almost black, eyes; those eyes, and the sensuous, loose largeness of her mouth, at odds with the Dresden-shepherdess features.

She looked down at me.

"What do you want?" I asked, but I knew.

She gave me a ten-shilling note. I nodded briefly, pocketed it and stood, folding the lid of the cash-tin over and locking it; I pocketed the key.

"Follow me," I said. I walked round to the cellar wall and opened the door into a room that had once stored files and office furniture, until the building above had been bombed a year or so earlier. Now it was filled with boxes, and bottles, many many bottles,

that gleamed in the dull light. There were cans of fuel too, too many. I never liked that they were down there. Here and there were long shapes wrapped in oilcloth; they included my own rifle – I preferred a pistol and doubted I would have need of it again, but someone would, for I had heard Clyde and Briscoe talking quietly to a man in an Irish accent a day or so earlier and I thought I could guess who he was. I had avoided him. If they found me I was in trouble, for sure; but not yet for treason.

In the corner was a bed. Clyde sat on it, stripped to the waist; he had been washing himself with a bucket. He had stopped no blows but his knuckles were raw.

"Clyde," I called out. "You got a lady visitor."

He stood up slowly and smiled.

"Well, ain't that a fact," he said. He turned to me. "Go watch that louse Briscoe," he said. "I'm gonna be busy."

I did not reply but nodded my head briefly, and turned away. There was an uneasy feeling in the pit of my stomach. And I wasn't wrong, was I. But I didn't sense the vileness of what would unfold. No, I didn't.

The dog opened his eyes. At the back of the house Caz and Tshering dozed in the deckchairs while Bazza busied himself in the kitchen, making lentil curry. It was a warm, soft afternoon. A bee bumbled by and there was a slight scent of roses.

*

Caz's friend Wendy was a surprise. Bazza had expected someone like Caz herself. Instead Wendy was a gentle creature with short glossy dark hair and dark blue eyes who wore a cottagey flowery dress that went from neck to knees and was gathered in under her bust, which was modest. She was somehow redolent of organic yoghurt. Bazza, and Tshering, wondered what had bought her together with a pot-smoking foul-mouthed menace like Caz. Richard, less tactful, actually asked.

"You don't seem an obvious match," he said, shovelling lentil curry onto his rice. Bazza poured him some Shiraz.

"Oh, we've known each other for a while," said Wendy. "Through my job." She was very well-spoken.

"Wendy is a nurse," said Bazza.

"Oh," said Richard through a mouthful of curry and rice. "Does Caz help you give people enemas?"

"No, no, silly," said Caz. She was about to pour herself another glass of wine then said, "These glasses are pathetic. Baz, are there any 250ml ones in the cupboard?"

"No, we broke the last one in the machine," said Bazza. "Poor Tshering cut his finger getting the glass out of the filter."

"Oh," said Caz. "Damn. Well, anyway, I don't help Wendy give people enemas. I pop into hospitals and old people's homes and things and help with the hard of hearing."

In the corner, the dog, who had been lying on his side, rolled onto his belly and raised his head. He looked at Caz.

"Caz's little brother can't hear," said Bazza, "so she learned British Sign Language."

"He manages very well now and is studying," said Caz. "I only use it when I see him, and I thought, seems silly to waste it really."

"Caroline, er Caz, is a huge help," said Wendy. "She really cheers everyone up. Not just the deaf ones, everyone likes to see her."

The dog rested his muzzle on his forepaws. *I bet she goes round getting all the oldsters stoned. Well not a bad idea really. I'd be bored to tears if I lived in one of those places. I'd be quite pleased if she came round and skinned up, especially in that transparent blouse.*

"It cuts both ways," said Caz. "I really like some of them."

"What do you find to talk to them about?" asked Richard, frowning. "The old people, I mean?"

"Oh, quite a lot," said Caz. "Mr Coulter, now, he's a scream."

"Oh, Mr Coulter," said Wendy. "He makes me laugh too."

"What does he do, old-time music-hall?" asked Richard.

"No, no, he's got ever so many stories," said Wendy. "He was an undertaker."

"Ah," said Richard. "Don't they all smell of pee though?"

"Oh, really, Richard," said Caz.

Tshering smiled. He raised his glass and took a sip of Shiraz. He was not wearing his robes tonight. Caz had tried to make him go to Primark, at least, and get a cheap pair of jeans, and then he'd confessed he had some. He also wore an old shirt of Bazza's and looked oddly anodyne.

The music stopped.

"What shall I put on next?" asked Bazza. He had been playing the Grateful Dead.

"Do you have any Paloma Faith?" asked Wendy.

"Er, I'm *sure* I can find some," said Bazza. He picked up the tablet beside his plate and toggled to the menu, and realised that besides Spotify, the icon for Porno for Android was clearly visible. He swept it aside with his thumb. A moment later Paloma Faith started to stream to the Bluetooth speaker on the sideboard.

"So when you talk to these people you really get something out of them?" said Richard.

"Oh, yes," said Caz. "Mind you, Wendy does too when she gives them enemas."

Wendy put her hand to hour mouth and giggled.

"Caz, don't be gross," said Bazza.

"Oh, do come on, Barnabas. You like it when I talk dirty," said Caz.

The dog raised his muzzle again and looked at her. *You're good. Wendy's good. Tshering's good. Bazza's all right really. Good people. Well, Richard's a pain. But good people, good people. What is it that I did not understand? What would they say if they knew what I was, what I have done, what I have seen.*

He let his muzzle fall to his paws once more.

"So who else do you like, 'part from Mr Coulter?" said Wendy.

"Old Mrs Donaldson's nice," said Caz. "I mean, she's not so lively, but she's always very considerate and kind, isn't she? I go when the doctor's there, and she's always so appreciative. She never could hear much but she could lipread but of course her sight's going now. And Mrs Gee's lovely."

"Mrs Gee is *wonderful*," said Wendy. "She's always so happy her life turned out well. Did you see her granddaughter's hubby the other day? Big strapping chap who just came out of the Army. Very smart in his uniform. I'll tell you what, I wouldn't mind."

"You naughty girl, Wendy," said Caz. "Yes, I love Mrs Gee. She's got this gentleness in her eyes. Of course, she shan't be long with us now I suppose. Don't seem to bother her."

"We are not afraid of the inevitable," said Tshering quietly. "We only fear what we have not accepted."

"She's a Christian, is Mrs Gee," said Wendy. "I suppose she's lived a good life and has nothing to fear."

"You mean she's not going to hell?" said Richard. "Do you believe in hell?"

"I don't know if I believe in imps and demons shovelling the damned into the flames," said Wendy. She thought for a moment. "I don't think it works like that. I think hell is within ourselves."

"Then religion doesn't matter very much, does it?" said Richard.

"Oh, but it does," she replied quickly. "It's still God's grace that saves us from damnation, whatever form it takes."

Didn't do much for me, did it. The dog yawned.

"Anyway, Buddhists don't believe in hell, do they, Tshering?" said Richard, smiling as he turned to the monk.

"This dhal is excellent," said Tshering. "It is not quite like that. What Wendy says about hell being within ourselves ...Well, we don't quite believe that either. But the mind can be the gaoler of the soul and prevent its transmission to a higher realm."

"But you said once," said Bazza, "that it is a mistake to believe that a soul transmigrates – at least, as an entity."

"In the sense of reincarnation?" Tshering

nodded and frowned. "Indeed, it is not so simple."

"But elements or fragments of the soul could do so?" asked Wendy.

"Yes, I believe that is so. The substance of the spirit may move to a new realm after death although it may not bear its identity."

"Hmm," said Bazza. "That sort of goes along the lines of what I was thinking the other day."

"You what?" said Richard. "Not going all mystical on us are you?"

"Not exactly," said Bazza. He was frowning too. He grasped the big 1.5-litre bottle of Shiraz by the neck and half-stood so that he could reach everyone's glass. "But I was reading one of Caz's essays for the course I teach..."

"Module 5.8," said Caz.

"Module 5.8. *Medieval cosmology and ontology.*"

"You are over my head," smiled Wendy. "I just empty bedpans."

"No, it is quite simple," said Richard, turning to her, "one's cosmology – one's understanding of the universe and the spheres; ontology – the nature of existence and thus of knowledge, of what we can know or not know." He looked at Bazza. "Is that a fair summation?"

"Yes," replied the other. "My own ontology is that I am a materialist – that is to say, everything is of physical matter."

"Indeed," said Richard. "So you cannot possibly believe in an afterlife. He can – " he nodded towards Tshering – "because a Buddhist's ontology does not exist on a solely physical realm."

"That is broadly true," said Tshering. "For us, reality must be sought in inner space. I could argue, if I wished – I shan't – that there is no external reality and that your perception is existence." He turned to Wendy. "As a Christian you believe in the redemptive power of faith and forgiveness. These are matters of the inner mind, the soul. You are not so far as you may think from our own world-view."

Doesn't matter. There's no inner space, chum. Nothing that I can do to control my fate. Forgiveness? Redemption? Come to hell.

The dog started to lick its balls.

"I love that dog but I do wish he wouldn't do *that*," said Caz.

"Oh, but they all do it," said Wendy. "I was born on a farm, remember." She turned to Richard, her elbows on the table, her fingers steepled before her mouth. "It seems to me," she said, "that you are probably a – what did Bazza say? – like him, you are a materialist. In philosophy, then, materialism says that everything is of physical matter, which would exclude an afterlife."

"Yes," said Richard.

"And any redemptive power of faith, or second chance."

"Oh yes."

She nodded slowly.

"Then why," she said, "do so many of us believe in it?"

"As an atheist and a materialist, I have no doubts on that score," said Richard. His voice was crisp; he sat a little straighter. "People have two reasons for believing in an afterlife. One is solipsistic and the other is judgmental."

"By solipsistic," said Bazza, "you mean that, whether he realises it or not, and even if he disbelieves it with his conscious mind, a man essentially perceives existence as a vehicle for himself, and cannot conceive of his own non-existence?"

"Precisely," said Richard. "You remember that shark Damien Hirst put in a tank some years ago?"

Wendy laughed. "How can I not," she said. "My dad thought it was hilarious."

"The title of the piece was *The Physical Impossibility of Death in the Mind of Someone Living.*"

"So it was," said Bazza. "Though I was never quite sure where the shark came in."

"So that is why we seek to believe in an afterlife, in a transmigration of the soul, reincarnation, heaven, hell, call it what you will. It is simply our colossal egos," said Richard, speaking with yet more assurance. "I am afraid Tshering would not agree."

"Actually Buddhism teaches that you should not see yourself as an entity in isolation from existence," said Tshering. He smiled slightly. "We may be more at one than you may suppose."

"Indeed. Whatever," said Richard. "Anyway, there is a second reason that people need to believe in the afterlife. They want to believe that evil will be punished."

"Well, why wouldn't we?" demanded Wendy. "What is wrong with that?"

"Do you believe," said Richard, "in the

existence of good and evil? I am not so sure I believe in a concept of pure evil, to be sure."

Oh, don't you. The dog stopped licking his balls, sat up and looked at Richard. *You stupid little shit. You silly little man in yourcreased jeans.* He lay down and emitted a low growl.

"What was that for, dog?" asked Caz.

"You don't have a name for him?" asked Wendy.

"Not really," said Caz. "Like Bazza says, he most probably had one, so it would be sort of rude to call him something else, wouldn't it. Anyway, don't worry about him growling. He does that, growls and yelps sometimes. We think he has bad dreams."

Wendy chuckled. "OK. Yes, I do believe in good and evil, sorry. Anyway, what makes you so sure that there isn't an afterlife of some kind, just because people *want* there to be? I mean, I would quite like to believe that Christmas will come, and oddly enough it does."

Everyone around the table smiled at this, except Richard.

"It is not possible for there to be an afterlife if there is no mechanism for the soul's transmission," he said, "and for a materialist, there isn't."

"I wonder about that," said Bazza. While the others had been talking, he had picked up the tablet from which he was streaming music and opened the browser. "Here we are." He held the tablet aloft before his face, having first checked that the Porno for Android icon was no longer visible. "Thus," he intoned, "while form changes place and circumstance, it itself cannot possibly be annihilated, since spiritual substance is no less real than material. So only outer forms change and are destroyed, since they are not things, but are 'of things'; they are not substance, but accidents and circumstances of substance'."

"What?" said Richard.

"You should know," said Bazza. "You're the materialist. That's Bruno in *De la causa, principio et uno*. Written in London. In 1584."

"Fuck," said Richard.

Wendy raised her eyebrows.

"Please forgive his profanity," said Caz. "He has just made an ontological connection."

"Who was Bruno?" asked Wendy.

"Giordano Bruno was burned at the stake in Rome in 1600," said Bazza. "He had offended the Church. Actually he had offended a few people, because he could be a pain in the arse. But he said two things that really freaked people out. First of all he said that the stars didn't revolve around ours but had planets of their own whizzing round them just like ours did."

"Wasn't that Copernicus?" asked Wendy.

"No. He had died just before Giordano Bruno was born, in fact, and Bruno would have known of his work – but Copernicus hadn't gone that far. All he said was that the Earth went round the Sun. Neither did he posit that the nature of other stars and planets was the same as ours. But Bruno went the whole hog."

"Was that the only reason why he was burned?" asked Caz. "There was more, wasn't there? Like what you just said. That everything is material – *everything*... including..."

"The human spirit," said Bazza. "It was of matter. Moreover he saw matter the way we today see energy; it can change its form but it cannot be destroyed."

"Hang on," said Richard. "Are you saying Giordano Bruno went so far as to say that the spirit was of the same matter as the remainder of existence, and that it could in effect survive death?"

"Yes to the first," said Bazza. "Not so sure about the second. If I were Bruno – or Tshering – I would perhaps say that the matter that comprises the spirit would survive but its form would change, and it would not retain its identity. But what if some proportion of its form did *not* change, or only partially did so? Bruno did not go that far. But why should one not?"

"My head is spinning," said Wendy. "What you are saying, in effect, is that there is a theory of existence – ontology you called it? – that is materialistic but does not exclude the existence, maybe even transmigration, of the spirit?"

"That is correct," said Bazza.

"Are you going to publish this?" said Richard.

"I will talk to Caz about it," said Bazza. "We may make it a joint paper."

"Will we?" said Caz. "You never mentioned that." She laid her hand on his arm and looked at him, smiling. He smiled back. Then he leaned forward and kissed her gently on the lips.

"This is fascinating," said Wendy, "and I shall put it to Father Jacques tomorrow after Mass. But I think he would have some questions."

"I expect," said Richard, "that Father Jacques would have Giordano Bruno burned at the stake."

"I doubt Father Jacques would burn anyone," said Wendy. "He is too busy with the food bank he runs with that nice Mr Ibrahim."

"Oh," said Richard. He looked deflated.

"But Bruno's – ontology? – materialism, call it what you will," went on Wendy. "It provides that the spirit might survive intact, even if this Bruno did not say that. What it does not do, is invest such survival with meaning. From what you have said, the spirit might or might not survive its owner's demise as a coherent form, rather as a seam of a rock might or might not remain whole when that rock was split with an axe; we are talking of pure chance, yes? There is no way that spirit could have moved to a state of grace before its destruction, or –" she nodded to Tshering – "acquired merit or karma."

"Of course the process is meaningless," said Richard, a little cross. "There is no God, no karma, no animated spirit."

"I am not sure Giordano Bruno would have concurred with that," said Bazza, and wrinkled his forehead. "He never denied good and evil; he simply suggested that since God, material or otherwise, was the largest form of matter, he or it would eventually subsume any evil."

"So a bad spirit would ultimately be absorbed by good?" asked Tshering. "Now we are a little closer to *my* cosmos."

Richard let the matter drop. He had just that noticed Wendy's breasts, though small, were pleasantly pointed.

"Anyway, now you have a name for your lovely dog," said Wendy.

"Eh?" said Caz.

"Bruno," said Wendy.

*

The guests had left by midnight. Tshering helped clear up then retired to his bedroom, to jot down some notes for a seminar he would give at the Art College the following week, and thence to bed. He seemed thoughtful, and looked at Bruno for a few minutes before patting him and fondling his ears. Caz thought she heard him speak to the dog. It sounded something like, "Remember, the way is hard." Then he was gone.

By this time it was nearly one. The air had thickened through the evening, and there was a close feel; suddenly there was a flash of lightning.

"Better get the dog out before it rains," said Caz, anxious.

"I think it's just summer lightning," said Baz. But then there was a thunderclap, distant but clear. "No, perhaps it's not," he said. "OK, Bruno. Nip out and do your business and I'll wait here to let you straight in."

The dog went down the garden.

"He seems depressed," said Caz.

"He does." Bazza poured a small glass of Averna and sat down on the kitchen step to wait. "He brightened up when we had that big argument though."

"What, about Giordano Bruno and reincarnation and that? Yeah, that was interesting. Mind you, Bruno's been a bit funny lately. He got a lot more friendly but it comes and it goes. Almost like he wants to be cheerful but something keeps ....intruding into his thoughts."

"Well, I suppose dogs have their worries too," said Bazza. He looked up at her. "Want an amaro?"

"Nah, I've done all right for tonight. I've got to get on with the dissertation in the morning.

See you in a few minutes."

Bazza sat with his glass and watched the lightning, more frequent now; the growls of thunder were still far off, but were coming closer. At length the dog's eyes caught the light as he emerged from the rhododendron bush and walked slowly back to the kitchen.

"How're you doing, then, dog?" asked Bazza. He took the dog by the ears and looked him straight in the eye. "Funny bloke you are sometimes, you know that?"

He paused for a moment.

"Love you though." He gave the dog a little pat on the neck, stood, stretched, and swilled the remnants of the liqueur from his glass.

"Bed," he said, pointing to the folding dog's bed that stood in the corner. The dog took his time as he walked to the bed, curled up and put his head down on his paws.

"Good dog," said Bazza as he turned the light out and gently shut the kitchen door.

No I'm not. If you only knew.

The dog slept very little. The lightning flashes that lit the kitchen became more frequent, the thunder closer and louder. It began to rain.

It was different that night, cold, but I think it was

clear. It was the sort of night when they would come over. Mind you we hadn't had that much trouble, not since May of the year before. After the nights got shorter they slackened off, and the next winter they never came back again, not in the same numbers. Busy in the East maybe. Then the first Americans came. Airmen mostly. They were all right. Not Clyde. I knew Clyde was a bad lot the moment I set eyes on him, and we'd both gone to ground and we both knew we were one step away from the glasshouse or worse. One difference though. I wanted to live, if I could, to make some money, to slip back after the war and get Sis out of that place. Clyde didn't want anything. Clyde hated everyone. Clyde already knew he was damned. Clyde was having a good time on his last leave from hell. Oh, I knew Clyde was bad. But I didn't know he'd do what he did that night.

So the last I saw when I left the store-room is she's slipped off her jacket and tilted her head back and run her hands down over her breasts and Clyde is standing, a great glistening monster of a man, and then he hits her with the flat of his hand, hard, across the cheek. A crack like the teachers' rulers. I wonder if they got the same feeling he did when they hit you like that. He stands back and the woman starts to unbutton her blouse. I want no part of this. I go out of

---

the cellar, pulling the door behind me, and see Briscoe stuffing his takings into his tunic pocket. "Turn the fucking lights out," I says. "Be just dandy if some fucking warden was walking past, wouldn't it. Just think what he'd find." Rat-face scowls at me and starts throwing the switches for the lights. Then the sirens start. "Thought we was done with that," he says. "Probably just a stray plane wandered over Croydon," I said.

But it wasn't.

Now, normally you got some warning. Some bugger must've been asleep on the job. Before long I can hear the ack-ack and there's a crunching sound. The ground shakes a little.

"Bit close that," says rat-face. He's looking pale. Rat-face always looks pale when the sirens go or there's a rozzer wandering about up top.

"Shut up. We got work to do," I say.

Together we start to lift the boxes of gin and bourbon that Clyde helped us liberate from a Yank canteen, PX as they call it, somewhere in Suffolk. He didn't tell us too much about how he managed that. "I arranged it," he said, imitating an English accent. A Yank 'fixes' things. We 'arrange' them. I had some idea of how he did it. An American corporal in the stores, compromised by having too many strange friends in the East End. An officer whose specialised tastes in women – or boys – had been brought to Clyde's attention. An English canteen hand whose taste for American luxuries made her accept too many nylons and Lucky Strikes, and was too deep in. A guard who came from the same town in Mississippi, where Clyde could arrange a beating for their father, a draft exemption for their kid brother. Clyde was enjoying this war, and just now he was enjoying it more than usual, I thought, as I heard the sounds of a slap and a cry from the back cellar.

"Don't like the sound of that," says Briscoe. "He's a fucking beast."

"Well I wouldn't spare your tears," I says. "Not for the likes of her. Let's get moving."

With two boxes each, we climb the cellar steps, pass through the double blackout curtains and pass into the cold late-winter air beyond. There are no lights on the ground, just a faint gleam here and there from the faint moonlight; but the slender pencils from the searchlights light the broken cloud cover and the flashes from the ack-ack are nearly constant. Over to the east there is a dull red light.

"Poplar," says rat-face. "Poplar or the docks."

I've paused to let my eyes adjust and I can just see the outline of the little Standard van with its canvas cover at the rear and its spare wheel sitting on the roof. I only drive it at night now. Otherwise someone would wonder about the paintwork. Number of times that van's gone from the Navy to the RAF to the Army and back again, and we even made it a Yank once with a nice big silver star on the side. Bit busy today so I haven't changed the number plates. Try to do that most days. In go the crates of bourbon and cigs and tonics.

"We promised 'em some meat," says Briscoe.

"We'll give them that side of pork we arranged out near Colchester."

"Reckon it's nearly off."

"You see them complaining?"

"Nope."

"Get it. I'll get the rest of the booze. I want to get this lot there afore the All Clear, while everyone's busy. We don't want someone looking at us too hard."

The side of pork did go in and it did smell a bit, I'll give him that. I felt a little blood through the greaseproof paper and gagged slightly. We felt our way back into the entrance to fetch the last of the bourbon. In the storeroom we could clearly hear the sounds from the inner cellar; the groans, rising to a crescendo, and the oaths, and the obscenities shouted out in Clyde's threatening growl and the woman's deep posh husky voice. I was just lifting the last crate of bourbon when I realised that Clyde's voice was louder. *You bitch, you fucking horrible bitch,* he was shouting, and then the woman's moans and oaths turned to screams and rose to a single terrible note that rent the air above the ack-ack and the thump-crump of the bombs far away. "For the love of God," said rat-face, whiter than ever, frozen to the spot, and I kicked open the cellar door – it wasn't locked – and saw Clyde raise himself from the woman's body, his naked torso shining with sweat, his trousers round his thighs. Below him the woman was spreadeagled, her skirt and knickers round her ankles, her blouse torn open. Her head hung over the side of the bed and seemed bent over to one side; her eyes were open; she twitched a little and her throat was a reddish-purplish colour. For a moment, there was silence, but for the sounds of the raid outside; then rat-face retched.

"She wanted it," said Clyde, looking down at the woman. "It was what she wanted. She was a horrible bitch."

"You fucking idiot," said Briscoe, recovering a little. "You fucking idiot. Do you know who she was?"

Clyde and I ignored him.

"You are the devil," I said. I could feel my voice

trembling. "You are Satan. You are fucking Satan."

He disengaged himself from the woman's legs and pulled up his trousers, threading the tongue of his belt through the buckle. Then he reached for his uniform jacket.

"So what are you?" he asked. "The angel Gabriel?" He put a slim cigar in his mouth.

"I'm better than..." I nodded towards the woman's body, then looked back at him. "I'm better than **this**."

"No-one's better than this," said Clyde. "I learned that kinda young, OK?"

"They'll come looking for her," said Briscoe. "People saw her. Here. It'll be all over the papers. They'll..."

"Shut up," said Clyde. He stood up and walked towards the door. "We'll move the body now. Where's the truck? Is it loaded?"

I didn't move.

"You're a demon," I said. "A demon."

"I asked you a question," said Clyde. He took out his Zippo to light the cigar; the flame shot up from below the lid. At the same time he advanced towards me. I backed towards the cellar door; Briscoe scrambled through it ahead of me. Clyde's arm was raised and I saw he was about to strike me. I leaped through the doorway behind Briscoe. Clyde paused to

---

light his cigar; then he made his move but his foot must have caught on a piece of rubbish on the floor, and he fell heavily. He got up. By this time I was several yards beyond the cellar door, and Briscoe several more. Then I heard an explosion nearer than the rest, then another nearer still, and realised it must be a stick. The ground shook and swayed. I staggered backwards. There was a groaning sound, and the floor above the cellar disintegrated and a beam fell on Clyde's neck and and his eyes opened wide in surprise, briefly; and he went where he belonged. His Zippo skeetered on its side across the floor, the wick still lit.

I tripped over Briscoe, who had been flung to the floor. Everything was covered in dust and there were several more beams that had fallen across the cellar and the store-room outside it. The wall to my right was bulging outwards, spurts of dust and dry cement coming from between the bricks, and I reckoned the floor above was about to collapse on top of us. There was a stink of gas and I realised that the explosion must have fractured a pipe somewhere in the cellar. "We need to get out," I said. "Briscoe, we need to get out." He was clearly stunned; he had stood up but was swaying back and forth.

Getting up myself, I saw that most of the petrol-cans had been flung across the floor. One of the lids must have been loosely screwed; there was a stink of petrol and I saw that a thickening rivulet was flowing towards Clyde's body. Not far from it was the Zippo, still burning.

"Now," I yelled, and seized Briscoe by the arm. Then he did react, and followed me up the stairs and into the fresh air. I kicked the door shut behind me. At that second, the place went up with the most almighty **whump**, the flames fuelled by a mixture of petrol, bourbon and gas. The door I had just closed blew out and I could see clouds of flame rolling up the stairs. Briscoe gave something between a whimper and a scream. "Get in the fucking van," I said. "At once." I could see the paint on the tailgate starting to curl in the heat. I pressed the ignition, but the engine turned too slowly. God in heaven. I seized the jack from the floor in front of the driver's seat – the van had failed to start the previous night and I had needed it then, so had left it where I could find it in a hurry. I went to the front of the van, remembered too late I had not checked the gearlever, prayed I had left it in neutral and found that I had. I engaged the dog on the end of the jack, slapped the crank with my right hand and heard the engine struggle into life. I pulled onto the street, nearly deserted but for the odd fire engine or ambulance that passed by with its bell clanging. We gathered speed, past a blimp lorry manned by WAAFs, past a gun emplacement, the barrel pointing at the sky, the crew craning their necks upwards. Down a side-street I glimpsed flames, and saw men and women with buckets, running, their heads down. An air-raid warden swerved in front of me on a bike. A knot of people stood, listless, beside a pile of rubble.

"Where we fucking going, anyway," said Briscoe. He was hunched forward, staring straight ahead, biting his nails.

"Essex or Hertfordshire," I said, gripping the wheel hard. "Or somewhere like that. I got to lay low for a while. And lose the van."

"What about this lot?" He indicated the cargo behind.

"I'll hide it. I'll sell it eventually."

"What about my share?"

"You'll get it."

"Maybe I don't trust you."

"You got no choice," I said. I jerked my thumb back the way we came. "They'll get into that cellar one day. I don't think they'll find anything very human. But what if they do? And they're going to want to know why the place went up like a Roman candle, too."

"Gas," said Briscoe.

"No. They'll find stuff. Fragments. Maybe even remains. You're going to report to your unit in the morning. And I'm going to scram."

Rat-face shut up then. He knew I'd never pay him and so did I. Dad and Sis needed every penny I could give them, every last rotten farthing.

We were somewhere between the City and the West End; I was heading north, and cannot have been far from Islington, when I swung round a corner to find our way blocked. Flames licked out from a mid-Victorian office building on our left, a few hundred yards ahead; white hoses snaked across the road and jets of water played across the flames. Two fireman were advancing towards the building, aiming a large hose. The fire shone orange in the wet asphalt. I stopped. An air-raid warden was running towards us; two more figures followed more slowly behind. I noticed a black Wolseley 14 standing to our right. It had a POLICE sign on the top.

"I think you'd best find another way, sir," said the warden. The reflection of the flames danced on his tin hat and the brass buckles of his canvas gas-mask holder.

I leaned out of the window. "I shall go back, and try and get round by way of Farringdon Road," I said. "Thank you."

Dog!

"One moment, sir." One of the coppers came up to me, his colleague just behind. "You won't mind if I have a quick dekko at your identity cards, will you?"

"By all means, constable," I said politely. I made to reach into my breast pocket. "Is there a problem?"

"There's been reports of some looting round and about and we just need to make sure of who's moving around, sir."

"Very good."

As he looked at my card I became aware of the other policeman looking at me through the windscreen.

"And yours, Corporal, if you wouldn't mind."

Briscoe leaned across me handed over his identity card. His was, of course, genuine. Mine was not but I thought it would pass muster in the gloom. The copper shone a torch on it.

"I'd be obliged if you'd put that light out, sir," said the air-raid warden.

"Now I really don't think Jerry's going to see my flashlight against that lot," said the copper. He jerked his head towards the burning building. There was a crash from somewhere within it, a floor collapsing perhaps. The copper didn't take his eyes from my identity card.

"You're a 2nd Lieutenant in the Ox and Bucks Light Infantry," he said conversationally.

106

"That's correct, constable."

"What brings you to London, sir?" he asked. His tone was easy, conversational. The second copper had shifted his gaze to rat-face, who fidgeted. I thought quickly. "I'm here quite often," I said. "Liaison duties."

"I see." The copper nodded. "Ox and Bucks are in Ulster as we speak, or so I believe."

"Indeed," I said, trying to think. For Christ's sake, why did I not know that.

"If you are on liaison duties, I imagine you have been at the War Office."

"I have been there, yes."

"Then why are you in a van with an NCO from Woolwich Arsenal?"

I could feel rat-face's fear.

"We have been examining a new American carbine," I said. "I'm afraid I'm not allowed to say very much."

"No. No indeed," said the copper. He handed back our cards. "A little unusual for an officer to be driving, sir. Is Corporal Briscoe unable to do so?"

"Corporal Briscoe cannot drive, constable."

"But you are normally stationed in Ulster?"

"That is correct."

"I wonder if I might see your travel warrant?"

"Oh." I looked around the cab. "I believe I left it in with my gas mask, which I forgot to bring with me."

"I see," said the copper.

The second one was standing, arms crossed, a foot or two from the Standard's mudguard. He spoke suddenly.

"What's in the back of the van?"

"Bits of machinery, mostly," I lied.

"You won't mind if we take a quick look, sir?" said the first copper.

"I'm afraid some of it is subject to security restrictions," I said.

"You can trust us, sir," said the second constable, his voice with more bite than the first's. "I don't think we'd know one end of a carbine from the other." He walked round towards the back of the van.

That's as maybe, I thought. You'll have less trouble recognizing crates of filched bourbon. In fact, the time has come, gentlemen, to bid you goodnight.

I let the clutch in and out then thrust the lever into first, revved up and banged the clutch in again. We shot off towards the snake's nest of white firehoses. I twisted the wheel as far and as hard as I could; the tyres screeched and the little Standard utility nearly stood on its side.

"You fucking maniac," screamed Briscoe.

I forced as much power as I could from the engine, heading back south towards the river. The sound of bells came from behind as the coppers recovered their equilibrium and gave chase in the Wolseley.

"You maniac," Briscoe repeated. "We're going to get caught, all right? I'd rather be in the glasshouse than fucking dead. Stop the blasted van."

"No," I said. I was surprised by how calm I felt. I glanced at him. "If we get caught, you go to the glasshouse for a few months." I looked in the mirror. The Wolseley was gaining on us, as of course it would. "You won't like it but one day you'll leave. But I'm a deserter, remember. If I go to the glasshouse they'll break every bone in my body. And then they'll give me a one-way ticket to Burma. Sorry, rat-face." I'd never called him that before. "I got nothing to lose."

"I got a wife," shouted Briscoe. "I got two little girls. I don't give a tinker's cuss if you got nothing to lose. Let me out of this fucking van."

I looked in the mirror again. I had turned a corner and the Wolseley could no longer see us, although it was only a few hundred yards behind. So I swung the little van to the right, into a side-street not far from Hatton Garden. Briscoe lurched across the car and into the passenger door, but the latch held and he lurched back the other way.

Up ahead there was a glitter of broken glass on the road. A shop window had blown out and there were bits of clothing and other items scattered across the road. A short way out from the pavement a mannequin lay on its back, the clothes blown off, its arms outstretched, its legs nowhere to be seen. There was still dust in the air and it seemed to me that whatever had happened, it had been but a few seconds earlier.

A young woman staggered into the street from the window. She swayed somewhat. She was not looking our way. I pressed the horn; she did not turn so I pressed the button again and again. Still she looked away from us. I realised she must have been deafened by the explosion and could not hear the approaching van. I swerved to the right of her, but at the last moment she moved again, into my path. I tried to swerve farther to the right and lost control. She did turn then, and saw us, and her eyes opened wide, for just long enough to register terror; then the van hit her and slammed her into the wall of a jeweller's shop, crushing her. The last I remembered of her was her head falling to one side, eyes still open, and then she fell forward onto the bonnet. Briscoe shot forward, and was caught half-in, half out of the windscreen, his

---

body cut almost in half as the van crumpled. I did not go through the windscreen; the rigid steel of the steering column had lanced into my chest and pierced my heart.

There is a moment's stillness, broken only by the sound of the police bell behind us; and then I am sinking down, down, sinking with the two people I have just killed, sinking also with that woman in blue, who was worthless but whose death I had no right to cause. I am sinking with Clyde, who knew nothing but hatred. I am sinking with Dad, who is wheezing and gasping to a lonely death on the parish. I am sinking with Sis, who I thought I could help with my stupid rackets, who'll be stuck now for the rest of her life in a living hell in a damp ward where no-one can hear when she tries to speak, no air, no sun, pissing the bed, punished for not eating her greens, slapped for touching herself, in prison forever, and I didn't want to meet good people, all they've done is show me how evil I am, evil, damned, terrible, a demon, and all a demon can do is howl, howl and spit, howl and the kitchen door burst open, and Bazza was there with his hands on the dog's ears, and the dog was still howling, and now Caz was there too and there were footsteps on the stairs as Tshering came down dressed in jeans and nothing else.

"What the hell happened to him?" asked Bazza. "What's the matter, Bruno? Are you in pain?"

"I think he's had a very bad dream," said Caz.

The dog let out one last, quieter, howl, then sidled up to Caz, his tongue hanging out, his bottom wiggling. He whined. Caz hugged him.

"Open the door, Bazza, and let's get him into the air," she said.

It was not yet six, but close to the longest day, and the garden was full of a delicate peach light. The air was clear and fresh. One or two clouds glowed pink from the rising sun. The dog lay down on the grass, front paws stretched out, head slightly to their right. He looked up at them, then looked away.

"Almost like he's in shock," said Caz.

"Yes," said Bazza. "That must have been a *very* bad dream."

He made them some coffee and its aroma drifted out of the kitchen. Caz sat with the dog. Now and then she stroked him; then his tail would wag a little, but he remained listless.

"We'll take you out for some lovely walkies later," she said. "In the park, by the lake. Would you like that? "

"Destiny is in town to take Clarissa to the speech therapist again today," said Bazza. "I promised I'd meet them at the Jolly Boatman at five. You don't have to come if you don't want to. But it would be nice for Clarissa. I expect we'll sit outside by the river."

"I don't think your sister wants to see *me*," said Caz.

"Well, we can always go together and you can take Bruno down to the lake."

"OK." She patted the dog. "That'll be nice, won't it? You'll feel better then." She looked up at Tshering. "You'll come, won't you?"

"Yes." Tshering stood in the doorway and looked at the dog, frowning, deep in thought.

*

They left the house at four, thinking to have a walk around the lake. Tshering was in his robes again, as he would go on to take a seminar in the university chaplaincy later. Now and then people glanced at him, and sometimes they smiled. It was a beautiful afternoon. The promise of the dawn had been fulfilled by a day of deep blue sky and low humidity, a gentle warmth touching the skin, a faint breeze clearing and quickening the air. As they walked through the park around the lake, Caz started to dance around and laugh and then she leaned down and held the dog gently by the ears and kissed him on the top of his head.

"You silly sausage," she said. "Do cheer up."

"He's still got that hang-dog look," said Baz.

"I think," said Tshering, "that there is much on his mind."

"What, like whether that Labrador bitch is going to be here today?" said Bazza. He chuckled.

Tshering, who had heard that story, frowned.

"No," he said.

Then his expression cleared.

"Such a day to be alive," he said.

The sun glittered off the surface of the lake. It was still high, but sinking, and there was a hill ahead of them. On it, perhaps a quarter of a mile away, there were three people, hard to see against the light. One was in a wheelchair.

"I do believe that's Wendy," said Caz, "and I think that's Mrs Gee."

"Then that bloke pushing the wheelchair is probably her hunky ex-soldier," said Baz.

"I should check him out," said Caz.

"Don't you even think about it," said Bazza.

"The practice of the dharma," said Tshering, "frees us from jealousy."

"Oh, don't be so damned *serious*," said Bazza, but then he looked at Tshering and saw that he was smiling.

"I'll go and say hello to Wendy and Mrs Gee, anyway." Caz turned up the hill. "You can sit here on the landing stage and enjoy the water."

They did so. The dog sat beside them. Caz approached the little group and heard Mrs Gee call out a greeting. She was quite small and very old but her eyes were bright and friendly.

"I do believe it's Caroline," she said. "How nice to see you, my dear." Her voice was easy to understand, but oddly modulated. Caroline smiled and greeted her in sign language. Mrs Gee turned to her grandson, who was pushing her wheelchair. "Ben, this is the nice girl who comes to see us and chat. Caroline, this is my grandson-in-law, I suppose you'd call him."

"Delighted," said Ben, smiling back. It was true; he was every inch a soldier, tall and broad-shouldered.

"Do you know what Ben and Julie told me this

morning?" said Mrs Gee. "I'm going to be a great-grandmother!" She used the mixture of speech and sign-language that she often used with Caz. "Isn't that exciting?"

"That's lovely, Mrs Gee!" Caz was smiling from ear to ear. She looked at Ben. "Congratulations. Do you know if it's a boy or a girl?

"Dunno," said Ben. He smiled. "We had the scan but we said as not to tell us, it doesn't matter. My mum's over the moon too."

"Do you know, Ben's mum is going to come all the way from Barbados, to help out after the birth," said Mrs Gee. "Isn't that wonderful?"

"Yeah. Not one but two grans fussing around. I'm ecstatic," said Ben.

But Mrs Gee wasn't looking at him. Her expression changed and she looked at the lake in the middle distance; a light breeze broke its surface and broke the sunlight into pinpricks on the water.

"Been a good life," she said quietly. "So horrid when I was young. And now I'm a great-grandma."

"What's that, Gran?" asked Ben. He engaged the brake on the wheelchair and came round so that she could see his lips moving. "What's that you're saying?"

"Been a good life," repeated Mrs Gee. "In the end. Bit hard when I was little." She looked up at Caz. "They thought you were stupid then, you see. If you couldn't hear. They didn't know what was wrong, they just thought I were touched, doolally. 'Course, I were nothing of the sort. No flies on me. But I didn't know that myself, did I. Not then."

She looked a little to the right of the water.

"What on earth is he?" she said. "He looks rather exotic."

"He's a monk," said Caz. "He's a friend of ours who's here to teach. He's called Tshering Thinley and he comes from the Himalayas. The bloke with the pigtail is my boyfriend Bazza. And the dog's Bruno."

The dog was a little ahead of Bazza and Tshering. He stopped, sat down, then raised his hindquarters, studying them. His tongue hung out over his teeth and his ears pricked up. He gave a little whine.

"What's he on about, our dog?" said Caz. She frowned. "Been well odd lately, he has."

"Smashing-looking dog," said Wendy. "Farm

dog, I reckon."

"Hey Bruno! Come and say hello to Mrs Gee," called Caroline.

The dog was about fifty yards away. He advanced towards them, then stopped again, whined, then came forward. He went straight to Mrs Gee. He whined and yelped several times. His ears had folded back against his skull again and he gave vigorous tail-wags. He went up to Mrs Gee and laid his chin on her lap.

"Isn't he lovely?" said Mrs Gee. "Friendly too." She stroked the dog's head with her ancient hand. He looked up at her, still wagging his tail. Then he got up on his hind legs, his front paws on the canvas of the wheelchair on either side of Mrs Gee's.

"Bruno," called Bazza, advancing towards them, a little short of breath. "You be careful of that lady."

"This is weird," said Caz. "He's been really gloomy lately. Hasn't had time for us humans, at all."

Mrs Gee leaned forward.

"You lovely dog," she said slowly. "You lovely dog." She put her arms around him and pulled him towards her. "You're a lovely, lovely dog, aren't you? Beautiful coat."

The dog licked her ear.

"Bruno, GET DOWN," said Bazza, appalled by her frailty.

Tshering held his hand out to him. "Wait," he said.

"You're gorgeous, aren't you?" said Mrs Gee.

For a moment they stayed like that, her thin arms around the dog's haunches.

"We better go I suppose, Gran," said Ben after a while. "Tea's at half-past."

"Down you get, Bruno," said Bazza.

He leaned down and put his hands under the dog's front legs, and lifted him gently down.

"I've never seen him like that with anyone. Not ever," said Caz. "Not even your sister's girl, and he really liked her."

The dog whined quietly.

"Tea," said Wendy firmly. The little group took their leave and went towards the lake. The dog wouldn't move but sat watching them go, his ears pricking up, and now and then giving a very low whine.

"Come on, Bruno, you silly sod, or we'll be late," said Bazza. When the dog wouldn't move, he crouched down beside him and started to unfold the dog's lead. Tshering reached his hand across once more.

"No," he said.

"What?" said Bazza.

"I don't know," said Tshering.

When the group were out of sight the dog stood and turned. He walked beside and a little ahead of them, his tail wagging gently.

"What was that all about?" asked Bazza. "I mean, nice old lady, but I've never seen the dog like that. I hope he didn't upset her, jumping up on her."

"I'm sure he didn't," said Caz. "Come to think of it, she did tell me they'd had a dog at home when she was little, a sort of rough collie, sounds a bit like Bruno really. Prince, I think she said they called it. He got trouble with its joints and her dad had to shoot him and she said she was really sad."

The dog stopped and looked back at her.

"And you look more cheerful, don't you, Bruno, you silly old bugger," said Caz.

The Jolly Boatman was at the top of the hill, above the point where the river flowed past the lake, separated from it by a walkway and a sluice-gate. They sat in the garden, Bazza fetching the drinks. The dog sat beside them. Now and then he went to one or another of them and rested his chin on their lap, wagging his tail gently. Once he jumped up and put his front paws on the bench and started to lick Bazza's ear.

"Whoaa," said Bazza. He laughed. "Now, no more nightmares, all right? Silly old mutt. And if you like you can sleep on my bed now and then. Long as your breath doesn't stink."

"You'll get hairs all over the duvet," said Caz.

The Boatman had a car park, but it was across the road. The road was busy in the rush-hour, but that had not quite yet begun, and although there was a steady stream of cars, they were some way apart.

When they had been there for a quarter of an hour Destiny's small grey Audi appeared with her at the wheel. It turned into the car park and she and Clarissa got out. Destiny walked around the car making sure the doors were locked, although the car had central locking.

Clarissa walked to the road. She was wearing the same simple dress she had worn a few days earlier. She saw Bruno, stopped and smiled, then turned to her mother. She called out something and her mother replied; they couldn't hear – a car was passing by. Then she looked left and right and started to cross the road, her mother some way behind her.

In the middle distance there was the sound of a motorcycle engine. The bike appeared at the end of a side-road and stopped, its rider looking right to see if there was oncoming traffic.

Clarissa was halfway across the road. She glanced back at her mother to see if she was following. Her mother called something, then realised the girl was too far away to read her lips, and made sign-language symbols. As Clarissa looked back at her, the motorcyclist, looking right but not left, pulled out and accelerated rapidly up the road. Then he saw the girl standing in the road, a hundred yards or so in front, not looking at him, staring instead at her mother in the car park; but of course she could hear the engine. When he realised that she could not, he braked, but it was too late. Still she stood there, until a dog appeared from the pub garden and launched itself across the road, and leaped up at her, pushing her with his forepaws. She jerked in shock and reeled backwards.

The front wheel of the bike struck the dog halfway down his back. There was a scream. The bike slewed sideways and the rider was flung across the carriageway. From the corner of his eye he could see a middle-aged man with a ponytail run towards the road. With him was what looked like a Buddhist monk. There was silence for a few pregnant seconds, then a terrible howling.

"Clarissa! Clarissa!" shouted her mother.

The girl sat up, her eyes wide open. She looked at Bruno and screamed.

"Are you all right?" Her mother wrenched the seated girl round by her shoulders and looked at her. "Are you all right?"

Clarissa nodded slowly. She looked back towards the dog. Bazza and Tshering were crouched beside him, the former with his hand on the dog's head, the latter holding Bazza by the shoulders.

"For fuck's sake! I'm hurt!" shouted the rider. His bike had fallen to the right and had dragged his leg backwards, and his knee was pure agony. Still lying on his side, he raised his visor, to see the man with the ponytail and the monk attending to the dog. "For God's sake, phone an ambulance!"

"Fuck off," said Bazza. Caz was crouching

beside him now. "Poor Bruno, poor Bruno," she was saying over and over again.

It was Destiny who collected her thoughts first. She opened her old fliphone and dialled 999. Clarissa was standing now, swaying. The dog was still howling, but more quietly now. Caz had gone very pale and Bazza was crying.

"We must get a vet," she said. "Get a vet."

"No," said Tshering. "Look at his back. It is broken. Let him pass over."

The dog howled one last time and whimpered. He looked at Tshering.

"The way is hard," said Tshering. "Sometimes it is too hard. But it is done now."

The dog seemed to understand. He looked at Tshering for a second or two more, and then his eyes closed.

Cars were stopping now, their brake lights coming on in a long line as they pulled to the side and their drivers got out. Someone took a shot of the scene on a cellphone. Someone else had draped their jacket across the motorcyclist, who was breathing heavily. Clarissa was standing on the pavement, her hands clasped together, shaking, but not crying yet. Bazza and Caz stood up slowly, holding hands. In the middle of the road the monk knelt beside the dog's body, intoning a prayer.

Also by Mike Robbins

Fiction

Three Seasons: Three Stories of England in the Eighties

A washed-up trawler captain. A sleek young businessman. And the Master of an Oxford college. Through these three characters, all beautifully drawn, Mike Robbins has created a vivid picture of the 1980s, a divisive era. *Three Seasons* is a book of three novellas, unconnected with each other, but all set in the south of England in the 1980s. These three stories are vivid portraits of a country and its people on the verge of change.

978-0-9914374-5-0 (paperback)
978-0-9914374-6-7 (e-book)

The Lost Baggage of Silvia Guzmán

When Silvia's country falls apart after a coup, she flees to London. Picked up by the police, she is dumped for weeks in a bed-and-breakfast with a crazy landlady, then rescued by cold intellectuals. She finds she is a nuisance to one side and a cause

to the other – but she has a surprise for everyone.
The Lost Baggage of Silvia Guzmán is a story of flight,
loss and the pain of exile. But it is also a sideways
look at liberal London – perceptive, caustic and
sometimes very funny.

978-0-9914374-0-5 (paperback)
978-0-9914374-2-9 (e-book)

Non-fiction

The Nine Horizons: Travels in Sundry Places
In the late 1980s Mike Robbins, a young journalist
in London, felt restless and decided to travel. Over
the next 25 years, he never really stopped. The
pieces in this book take the reader from rural Sudan
to the headwaters of the Amazon, across Bhutan on
a motorbike, into the ancient souk of Aleppo, to the
steppes of Central Asia and finally to New York.
Along the way there is Ethiopian gin, a sex tourist
in Moscow, Kyrgyz women in cycling pants, echoes
of slavery in Brazil and a surreal toilet in Brussels.
The Nine Horizons is an anarchic snapshot of a
troubled but beautiful world in transition.

978-0-9914374-1-2 (paperback)

978-0-9914374-3-6 (e-book)

Even the Dead Are Coming

In 1987 the author, a 30-year-old London journalist, decided on a change of lifestyle and signed up for two years as an overseas volunteer. Some weeks later he found himself standing with his luggage in the middle of a featureless baked-earth plain in Eastern Sudan. It was over 100 deg F in the shade. And there was no shade. This is a personal account of two years living and working in a surprising, sometimes inspiring, country.

978-0-5780356-9-7 (paperback)
978-0-9914374-4-3 (e-book)